Frog Legs

SHORT STORIES ABOUT LIFE

WAYLAND BRYANT JACKSON

JTC

JACKSON-THOMPSON CONSORTIUM

FROG LEGS

Printed in the United States of America

Second Print Edition January 2023

Cover Art by Leigh Jackson

Published by:

JTC

Jackson-Thompson Consortium

2885 Sanford Ave SW #32684

Grandville, MI 49418-1342

Attn: John Thompson

https://waylandjackson.com/

Library of Congress Cataloging-in-Publication Data is available upon request.

ISBN 979-8-9876789-0-9 (Paperback)

ISBN 979-8-9876789-1-6 (eBook)

Acknowledgments

My deepest gratitude to the editor,
Holly Thompson,
who worked tirelessly to bring this work to fruition,
and to so many others along the way,
an encyclopedia could not contain all their names,
including but not limited to
sixteen brave souls whose names go up in lights
for having dropped everything
to preview FROG LEGS:

⌘

. . . Rich Lagomarsino . . .
. . . Steve Cleary . . . Joanna Cox . . .
. . . Carol Cromarty . . . Peter France . . .
. . . Sylvia Banuelos . . . Ronda Ramsel . . .
. . . Jeff Cates . . . Laurence D. M. Marshall . . .
. . . Rhonda Herb . . . John Thompson . . .
. . . Jean-Paul Lor . . . Glynna Billings . . .
. . . Jonni Pettit . . . Larry Norton . . .
. . . Deborah Homan Still . . .

⌘

~ No greater compliment could be paid ~

Contents

" *. . . a time to weep . . .* "

ECCLESIASTES 3:4

Our little neighborhood gang had tired of Cowboys and Indians. We had played Restaurant, exchanging Fool's Gold from the arroyos near our home for cold biscuits from the kitchen and carrots and tomatoes from the garden. Having no shade near the woodpile where we stacked logs to make seats meant we could not play School.

Huddled beneath purple-blossomed Chinaberry trees, someone said, "What do you think's in the hen house?"

My sister ventured in among the perches and nests and soon returned with an egg cupped in her hands. We huddled around like students in a surgical theater, while Valura, our leader, broke open the egg. (Having a second toe longer than her great toe, her mother instructed her, was a sign she was destined to be the boss in her family.)

The contents of the egg spread over the ground in the center of our circle. We leaned in, staring, when suddenly, a wrenching, sulfuric odor hit us. We leaped back, grabbed our noses, and made awful faces. After we recovered, we decided what lay before us were the earthly remains of an unborn chick. Without question, it deserved a proper burial.

Funerals were a mainstay of the social life of our village, so we knew what to do. We got the Diamond matchbox from our kitchen for a coffin, and Bobby got Papa's shovel from the toolshed. Along the way, Helen gathered a handful of tiny white and purple wildflowers, as Valura led us, single file like a desert caravan, across the grass to the alley behind the barn on a hot July afternoon.

The ground was dry and hard, so each of us took a turn with the shovel, whose handle reached above our heads. The minute the hole was deep enough, we placed the matchbox in the grave and made a mound using the excavated dirt.

Helen bound two sticks together with stems of Johnson grass to form a cross for one end of the grave, and she placed her bouquet in the center. We made a circle around the grave and bowed our heads. I said the only prayer I knew:

> "Now I lay me down to sleep,
> I pray the Lord my soul to keep,
> And if I die before I wake,
> I pray the Lord my soul to take."

We sang heartily: "In the sweet by and by . . . " Eventually, all must die, but with any luck, we'll meet again "on that beautiful shore."

We turned to look for the nearest shade when someone said, "No one has cried." We had forgotten this essential element. So, we got back into a circle and began trying to cry. But tears on demand didn't come naturally to any of us.

So, we agreed to go around the circle, each one slapping the person on their right one after another until someone cried. It's hard to slap a friend, so the slaps were more like pats.

Forgetting that Valura, older and taller than me, was on my left, I shouted, "If we're gonna do it, do it and get it over with!"

Valura's arm flew through the air like lightning from a cloudless sky. Her hand blazed a trail across my face and left my jaw stinging. Someone had finally cried, and I ran to the house to tell on Valura for hitting me.

Frog Legs

This is not a typical sports story.

For a city of half a million, even a junior high volleyball championship is a big deal. But since junior highs didn't allow students to attend away games, Teacher Daniel Hunt would be his team's lone supporter. He drove eight miles across town and arrived fifteen minutes before the team on the yellow school bus. He parked behind three Mercedes on the south side of Longfellow Junior High.

Entering by a gate in the chain-link fence, Hunt climbed to the top of the metal risers flanking the outdoor court. He settled his tall, lanky frame near the top, next to Longfellow parents dressed in colorful, casual attire, chatting among themselves. Below him waved a sea of broad-brimmed hats. On either side of him, eyes were secure behind dark shades. Cheerleaders wearing an embroidered "L" on their uniforms filled the front row.

The hiss of the bus braking announced the arrival of the Tioga team. Dressed in faded purple and gold uniforms, the team, with Coach Norris, poured out onto a sizzling sidewalk. Chia, the shortest boy on the team, brought up the rear.

Spectators and cheerleaders gave the visiting Tioga team a quick nod, but when the Longfellow boys paraded out of their locker rooms in bright, new uniforms with matching tennis shoes, they raised a rousing cheer. The Longfellow boys fanned out and began warming up, leaping, spiking, placing the ball with confidence in the opposite court, and putting a mean spin on overhand serves.

The Tioga team spiked and set well, too, but the Longfellow boys were taller and had the home-court advantage. Their cheerleaders, cute to the nails, went through practiced routines: arms up, arms down, jump, and spin, pompoms shimmering. They beamed with precise smiles radiating Longfellow enthusiasm.

Tioga Coach Ed Norris, a science teacher, and former pro basketball player, stood like a sentinel, watching his boys warm up. They were set to play the only other undefeated team in the city. When one of his team made a mistake, Norris's style was to let the boy take responsibility for it without a negative word. All the boys on his team got playing time.

With courts chosen by a coin toss, teams gathered around their coaches for a pep talk. Both teams joined hands and shouted. Cheerleaders took their seats as teams poured onto the court. A blast from the referee's whistle and play began.

───────────⟨∞∞∞⟩───────────

T he first serve, by Longfellow, was an ace. The Tioga team looked puzzled, like, *Who should have gotten that?* When Tioga finally managed to return the ball, Longfellow sent it back again. Poised and cool despite the heat rising from the court, the taller boys ran up eight unanswered points, halfway to a win before Tioga got its first score.

The first game ended, 15 to 5. Longfellow spectators and cheerleaders, only one game away from the championship, broke out in rousing shouts, anticipating another easy win. Hunt wondered if some of the Longfellow parents might leave since their team seemed to have the trophy sewn up. On the other hand, he had never seen parents leave with their kids so near an important victory. Hunt considered leaving, but he too stayed, intrigued by the glint in Chia's eyes. Chia was enjoying the game despite losing.

⸻

T hough short, Chia came well-equipped for a sport that requires a player to maneuver an eight-foot-high net. Near the door to Hunt's classroom at Tioga sat a box containing homemade reed balls about 6 inches in diameter. On the lawn outside the door, before school each day, Chia played Qtaw, a traditional Hmong game with some similarities to volleyball, the exceptions being that players may not use their hands, and players do a handstand to spike the ball with their feet.

So, when Coach Norris announced tryouts, Hunt mentioned the idea of joining the volleyball team to Chia. Chia hesitated. Putting himself forward was a notion unfamiliar to him. Still, he showed up. Coach Norris wondered about his size. However, when Chia took his turn in the rotation, his quickness and jumping ability impressed Norris. Chia ran drills as well as most of the boys, so Norris had no misgivings about putting him on the roster.

⸻

O n the scorching tarmac, the score stood at thirteen to ten in Longfellow's favor near the end of the second game. They needed only two points to seal the victory and be off to a pizza party.

Spectators were on their feet, shouting along with the cheerleaders. The boy opposite Chia spiked the ball and barely missed Chia's head, putting Longfellow only one point away from victory.

Then, as will happen, the momentum shifted. Tioga began to score, moving up point by point, finally passing their opponents. With a little luck, skill, and consistency, the Tioga boys fought to a sixteen to fourteen win, making a third game necessary. A puzzled silence fell over the spectators.

While the Longfellow coach had burnt up a lot of his team's energy using his best players without a break for the first two games, Norris continued to rotate his players. His face showed neither delight nor apprehension. The perspiration on his forehead could have been nothing more than the weather. Sounds from the fans had grown sporadic. Only individual shouts punctuated the silence.

When the referee called for the third game to begin, the Tioga boys gathered around Norris, who towered over them. After he said a few words, hands overlapped, and they gave the traditional shout. The boys moved to the other side of the net, reminding Hunt of stories Chia told about his family fleeing from defeat to safety across the Mekong River after the Vietnam War.

I n the third game, the lead went back and forth. Longfellow cheerleaders, still in perfect time, encouraged their team, but spectators seemed concerned, and the team's air of superiority had given way to frustration. Perspiration dotted the shirt of the player opposite Chia. His jump had lost its snap. When he spiked, a grimace indicated he was digging deep for stamina. When Chia blocked his spike, the tall boy's face contorted. With a rumpled head of hair, he glared at Chia and scraped his foot across the asphalt a couple of times like an animal eager to charge.

Looking at him, Hunt thought, "A couple of horns and a flashing tail, and that kid would look right at home in a bullfighting ring."

When the tall boy tried to block Chia's spike, at the very last second Chia would send the ball in a different direction, or he barely tipped the ball, so it dribbled down the other side of the net making it difficult to return. When Tioga moved to only one point away from defeating Longfellow, an ominous silence fell over the unbelieving fans. Hunt shook his head, finding it hard to believe what he was seeing, and wondering what was going through Chia's mind.

The day following the match, students came after school to play board games in Hunt's classroom before going home. Chia was without a partner, so Hunt offered to play him a game of chess. They moved two desks to face each other, laid out the board, and Chia opened with his knight. "How was that third game yesterday?" Hunt asked.

Chia hesitated. He asked, "Do you really want to hear about it, Mr. Hunt?" suggesting something unusual had happened. After Hunt assured him he did, Chia began to describe the scene.

The player opposite Chia, under his breath and with just the hint of a smile, said, "Frog legs." At every opportunity, he looked Chia straight in the eye and repeated, "Frog legs."

The sounds of English l's and r's were still jumbled in Chia's brain. He finally figured out the words the boy was repeating, but he still couldn't understand why the boy was saying them. Was there something bad about frogs' legs? They're strong. They enable frogs to move on land and in the water. They're good to eat.

Finally, Chia sensed the boy was saying something about Chia's body. It had never occurred to Chia there was anything remarkable about his body, certainly nothing he should be ashamed of. Gradually he began to think of his legs in a way he never had before.

As the taunts continued, Chia sensed the boy's embarrassment at losing a volleyball championship to a team from across town composed mostly of interlopers in his country. But that knowledge didn't lessen the sting of the words. "Frog legs," like the blows of an ax, echoed again and again. When the game point was called, Chia was in the center of the net, face to face with his tormentor. The ball came to the right. Chia's teammate set it up for him. As his opponent leaped to spike the ball, he took one last stab, "Frog legs."

Hunt wanted to say, "You should have stepped under the net and let him have it!" Instead, he said, "Why didn't you push back? He would have deserved anything you gave him."

"I wouldn't do that," Chia said without emotion. "Someday that boy will remember what he did, and he'll feel sorry about it."

Hunt was beginning to boil. He wanted Chia to understand: If someone does something underhanded, speak up. Demand your rights.

"Chia," he urged, "unsportsmanlike conduct is dirty. No good coach wants to win like that. You should have told your coach or the referee. The boy needed to be called on it. That's only fair."

Chia said, "Being fair makes people equal." With eyes still lowered, he continued as if instructing a simple child. "I don't want to be equal to that boy. I don't choose that."

Hunt saw the logic. Responding to bad behavior with bad behavior would make two people equal—equally bad. He had heard of returning good for evil but had never taken it seriously. Now, he was seeing it demonstrated by a 13-year-old boy!

Chia continued, "I waited until the boy jumped to block. As he started down, I put the ball between his open arms."

When the winning ball landed in Longfellow's court, the Tioga team cheered, which they quickly muted, as Norris had taught them. There was no crowing, and there was no ceremony. The trophy would come in the mail. The spectators milled about. Longfellow players and fans wondered, *Was the pizza party still on?* The cheerleaders faded quickly as the two teams passed by in a line, each player giving the boys on the other team a high five.

Ed, still with a sober face, shook hands with the Longfellow coach and the referee. The Tioga boys picked up their gear and headed for the bus. As the team filed past the bleachers where Hunt waited, Chia looked up. Hunt thought he saw just the trace of a smile.

"Best if used by . . ."

One month away from my senior year at Hathaway High, I saw on my friend Mark's computer that a male reaches his sexual peak at age 17. In less than eight months, I'd be past my sell-by date. I'd had wet dreams, so I was convinced the real thing must be like crossing the finish line at Splash Mountain.

No one ever offered me a movie contract, but I'm clean and neat, and I take care of myself. I could grow a beard but that's not my style. My skin is clear. I guess my best feature would be my eyes. According to an expert (my mom), when I smile, my eyes sparkle.

That's why I never smile at 7-Eleven. If I'm the only customer, I pay and get out fast. The clerk looks at me like I'm a 16-ounce steak she could take in one bite. She's real old, like 25 at least.

I don't have a lot of friends at school. As a kid, I liked my paper route because I rarely had to talk to a customer. In Scouts, I got a lot of badges by choosing projects I could do mostly alone. I figured I could approach getting laid the same way, with steps and everything, the first step being to find a girl, and she didn't have to be the Homecoming Queen.

W hen school opened, I zeroed in on my 11 o'clock English class. If I saw a likely candidate there, we could get acquainted at lunch. Finally, I got the list down to three. Ariana was a blond who really filled out a sweater. Natasha was pretty, especially her dark hair, and she dressed nicely. She always looked good even after P.E.

The third girl on my list, Emily, had auburn hair with soft curls surrounding her face like a frame. She looked like she was very much in charge of herself, independent and sure. I got the impression she could handle herself in any situation. The more I watched her, the more I thought, with her cooperation, my project might move as smoothly as an ocean liner in the night.

When Emily read her essay to the class, she held our attention as if she were announcing school was dismissed for the rest of the day. That's when the idea hit me. I was having trouble with my essay. If I could get her to help me with my writing, I could kill two birds with one stone, so to speak. Often, she had lunch in the cafeteria, but sometimes she brought a sack lunch and ate at a table on the quad. I started bringing my lunch every day, ready to engage at the first opportunity.

I debated about how to begin:
  • "Emily, I'm Jason. Would you be willing to have sex with me?" Hardly.

  • "Emily, let's get better acquainted so I can get you to do it with me." See how messed up I was?

Unfortunately, I didn't have many places to go for help. Certainly not Mark. He was as bad off as I was.

T he aroma of cinnamon hit me as soon as I opened the front door. In the kitchen, I got a tall glass of milk, took a stool, and helped myself to a warm Snickerdoodle cookie. I tried to sound casual, like it was no big deal. "Mom, there's a girl in my English class I want to meet. I don't know what to say."

"This is news." She continued rolling the cookies in cinnamon and sugar. "What's her name?"

"Emily."

"Tell me about her." She put the pan in the oven and set the timer.

"She read her essay to the class. It was good. I'm thinking she might help me with mine. Plus, I think she's cool." No way would I tell Mom what I had in mind.

I know you shouldn't describe a smile as a "knowing" smile, but that's the look I saw on Mom's face.

"How about being upfront, the direct approach? Ask her if she has time to help you. If she doesn't have time or doesn't want to, she can say no without seeming rude. And if she says yes, I guess you'll need to have a place in mind—the library."

That would totally work.

⸙

At the end of class on Tuesday, Emily took a paper bag from her backpack. Lunch in hand, she went to the quad, and I followed. As soon as she was seated at a table, prepared for any response, I walked over and forced myself to speak. "Hey, Emily." She looked up and squinted. She didn't smile, and she didn't frown—more of a questioning look.

"I'm Jason. We have English together. Mind if I share your table?"

"Okay," she said. I got the feeling she was surprised, maybe pleased. She unwrapped plastic utensils and unfolded a napkin without looking at me, spread dressing on her chicken salad, with croutons no less, and put a straw in her juice. I got out my egg salad sandwich, a carton of milk, and a large Snickers bar.

"Emily, the essay you read in class, I've tried to write like that, but I don't even come close. I wonder if you've got time to help me figure it out." It had to be a line she hadn't heard before.

She paused. "I don't know. I've got a full load, and I have work to do at home." She scanned me like airport security, looking directly at me, not blinking.

"I want to get into a good college, and I know this will help my admissions packet." I added my special smile, hoping my eyes did their thing.

"I'll think about it," she said. I wanted to check off step one, but I wasn't home free, yet.

During the next few days, I felt like she was checking me out. So, if the teacher asked a question and I thought of something to say, I made myself speak up. I wanted her to know I wasn't an idiot.

I got to bed late Thursday night, so on Friday, I had trouble staying awake in fourth period. The bell startled me. I looked up from my desk, and there she stood. "Jason," she said, "Let's have lunch." We agreed to meet in the school library.

⁂

Waiting just inside the library with one eye on the door, I foraged around in my brain for something to say, but I wasn't happy with any of my ideas. To me, small talk is the noise people make when their brain is idling, but I had to start closing the gap between "help me with my essay" and getting laid. I only had six months left, but I didn't want to spoil it by rushing things.

When she came through the door, the room seemed just a tad brighter. I gave her good eye contact and kept up my smile as we wove our way to a small table near the computer lab. When we sat down, I moved my chair closer. She gave no sign she noticed. We dropped our backpacks on two empty chairs and took out notebooks. "How can I be more persuasive?" I asked.

She said, "It helped me to get the basic framework in mind before I did any writing."

"So what framework are we talking about?"

"The outline we learned in debate club last year: State your idea, think of three arguments in favor of your idea, and explain why you think they're good reasons. Next, list three things people might say who object to your idea. Explain why their arguments are weak or flawed, then wrap it up." Her explanation was a lot clearer to me than what our textbook said, perhaps because it was shorter and more to the point. She could have taught the class with no problem, I thought.

"Do you have something you want to write about?" she asked. Premarital sex crossed my mind, but I said, "Anything except politics and religion."

"I wrote about immigration because my doctor was a professor at a teaching hospital in India, but because of our laws, he can only practice general medicine. Instead of teaching other doctors, he's giving flu shots."

While Emily continued to talk about the Sikhs and immigration, I tried to think of three good arguments that would persuade Emily to do it. First, I said to myself, it's a natural behavior.

"It's a natural behavior, isn't it?" I heard Emily say.

"*Natural behavior!*" I choked. I must have looked like a deer caught in the headlights. I took a big gulp.

Emily said, "It's natural, isn't it—to resist what we don't understand, to feel threatened by it?"

I took a deep breath. "Oh, yes. Natural." I was having trouble keeping 'natural behavior' in the cranial part of my body.

I made notes on the outline she gave me to let her know I was paying attention, then it was time to leave.

"I won't be able to work with you again till next Friday," she said. "I've got schoolwork and chores at home. Write up something. We can look at it next week."

I walked her out to the bus stop. Her mother drove up in a Lexus, and Emily got in. As the car merged into traffic, the thought occurred to me. I could offer to help her with chores at home, and while there, scout out the situation. We would need a place, and a house is a place.

At lunch Monday, I said, "Emily, since you're helping me, could I help you? Need a strong back for any of your jobs at home?"

"I'll check with Mother and let you know."

I waited with Emily every afternoon for her mother to arrive. On Thursday, we were at the bus stop for about 45 minutes and her mother didn't show. Emily tried to call her mother, but Emily's battery was low, so I gave her my phone. It turned out her mother was working late and had tried to call to tell Emily to take the bus home.

"I always have a bus pass," she said, "for emergencies."

"Then if it's okay, I'll go with you." She didn't disagree.

The bus was full, so we held our backpacks on our laps. After a few miles, the crowd thinned out, and we put our books in seats on either side of us. I laid my hand at my side between us. Emily placed her hand lightly on mine. Suddenly, I felt like I had been connected to a 220-volt line. I slowly moved my hand on top of hers, and the electricity continued. I glanced at Emily, looking straight ahead, her face serene, untroubled.

Emily's house was about a block from the bus stop. Her mother wasn't home, and she hadn't mentioned a dad. If the house was empty, it was an open invitation. When I passed her backpack to her, I gave her a little peck on the cheek, and that set off the electricity again. I left without going in, but I remembered the smell of her hair. I smiled all the way home. I couldn't help it. People on the next bus probably thought I was high on something.

T hree weeks into the semester, the biology labs were overflowing with too many students for the stations available. A noontime lab was opening. I asked Emily to be my partner. She agreed, and we arranged our schedules to do a lab during lunch and eat later.

Luck was on my side. Shortly after the lab opened, we were dissecting frogs. Soon the sex organs would come into view. When we got to them, I looked at Emily and shrugged slightly. "It looks like everybody does it," I said. "Instinctive, isn't it?"

"You're right," she said, "with one exception."

"Yeah?"

"Humans. We're exceptions. We have instincts, but we also can make choices, choose a person, a time, and a place."

I liked the sound of that.

Then she added, "We can also say no."

"Clean up time," the teacher announced.

"Can we talk about this later?" I asked.

"If you like." She was quite casual about it. If she was interested at all, she hid it well.

———⨯⨯⨯———

T he next step had to be a date. But I had no idea how to ask, where to go, how to act, or what to do about transportation. A movie? Should I suggest one that's R-rated and one that's PG, to give her a choice?

Back to the drawing board. "Mom, I want to ask Emily out on a date, but it's complicated. Can you help me?"

I saw just the hint of a smile. Mom wasn't laughing at me. She was pleased. "Your first date's a big deal. You can't know exactly what to do and say. I bet Emily wants pretty much what girls have always wanted. Respect. Kindness. Thoughtfulness."

"I can't put on a show for her."

"You don't have to. You're thoughtful and respectful. In your own way, you're kind. If you keep Emily's feelings in mind, you'll be okay."

That was nice of Mom to say those things, but generalities weren't much help.

I went for it. The worst that could happen to me would be to crash and burn—still a virgin. "Emily, how about a movie, you know, a date?" I held my breath, braced for a knockdown. If she said, "No" or "Let's just be friends," I would be disappointed, but anything above that would be a win.

She said in a calm voice, "Cool."

That was all the good news I could take for one day. I never dreamed someone could make me feel so good and confused at the same time. Here was a person, not one in a crowd, a real individual who was letting me in, opening up to me. Was it possible I could open up and be myself with her?

Then came my next surprise. "You get the tickets," she said. "I'll pay for the snacks."

What was I supposed to say? I said thanks.

"I'll talk to Mother. She'll give us a ride—if that's okay with you."

"Great." Transportation solved. If she drops us off, we can be alone in the theater.

I don't usually give much thought to what I wear. My clothes are school clothes, except for my funeral clothes. I call them that. Whether it's my funeral or someone else's, those are the clothes I'm wearing. However, I wanted to look nice. Mom bought me a new T-shirt with the logo of my favorite team, the Denver Broncos. That's all the dressing up I could tolerate.

I honestly can't tell you the name of the movie we saw. I had other things on my mind, beginning with Mrs. Bradshaw picking me up. I didn't know whether to sit in the front, with Emily in the back, or sit in the back, with Emily upfront, or both of us in the back, like her mother was a taxi driver. Turns out, I didn't need to worry. Emily was in the back, and she opened the backdoor for me.

"I'm glad to meet you, Mrs. Bradshaw. I'm Jason," I said as I got in. "Thanks for giving us a ride." She nodded. When we arrived at the theater, as she let us out and drove away, I thought *She might not be so accommodating if she knew my ultimate goal.*

The theater was filling up quickly, but we got there in time to get good seats in the center, near the back, but not all the way back. Emily put her sweater in my seat to save it for me and slipped some cash into my hand. The line at the snack bar was long.

Thinking I could carry two sodas without a drink holder, I left the snack bar juggling two 20-ounce sodas and a bucket of buttered popcorn. When I got back to the theater, the trailers had begun, and the lights were dim. I finally found the right row and started across. The movie began as I was maneuvering around knees and stepping over feet while balancing the snacks.

About two seats away from Emily, I stepped on a woman's toe. She screamed, jumped up, and elbowed me into a freefall. I tossed the popcorn to free my hands to stop my fall. The guy in front of me jumped up and grabbed the sodas, saving several people from getting Pepsi-d. Everyone nearby got "corned." One guy tossed a kernel in his mouth and yelled, "Thanks! More butter next time!" I fell into my seat, and Emily was laughing. The man handed us our drinks, and nobody got mad.

The backs of the seats were too high for me to put my arm around Emily but reaching around a cup holder was no problem. Her hand was soft and warm. She laced her fingers through mine and squeezed. It was hot wire time again. I felt like I was blushing all over.

As we came out of the theater, Emily's mother drove up almost instantly, as if she had been parked somewhere watching for us. Remembering the vibes from Emily in the theater, I would like to have kissed her goodnight when I got out. But I didn't feel like trying it with her mom around.

The next day at school, I asked Emily if I could help with chores around her house. She said, "Not really. I'm not sure my Mom likes you."

"Where did that come from?"

"In her mind, if you need help with what she thinks is a simple assignment, that's strike one. Plus, she wants my friends to be people who know the college they're going to and are sure of getting in. She was glad I paid for the refreshments at the movie. That way, I don't owe you."

I didn't know how to respond. "Does your mom choose your friends?" I had heard of helicopter moms.

"I never thought about it. Yeah, I think she does." She was silent for a moment. "I can't totally ignore her opinion."

"What about your dad?"

"We don't see much of him. He's stationed in Germany. But, he'd back Mother. He respects the chain of command."

"So, what's next?" I asked.

"How about we hang out at the game Friday night?"

"Cool," I said. I wouldn't deliberately diss Mrs. B, but I was glad she wasn't *my* mom.

The game was the annual rivalry between Hathaway and McClendon High. There was a lot of yelling. A small fight broke out near the entrance, but security handled it.

Bands from both schools took turns blasting out quick-step marches, and the Pep and Cheer teams were in their usual frenzy like they were all on a controlled meth trip. Our side of the stadium looked like it had been bathed in green Jell-O, and the McClendon side was decked out in yellow.

Before the teams came out on the field, Emily came through the gate with a group of her friends. Seeing me, she peeled off like a fighter pilot breaking formation.

I greeted her with, "You can have any snack you want, but you'd better pay for your own, otherwise, you'll *owe* me." I laughed to make sure she knew I was teasing.

We climbed to the top row of the bleachers. I put my arm around Emily without any trouble. She seemed to like that, so I took her hand in mine and held it. In addition to being smart and pretty, she was breaking loose a bit, defying her mother, even secretly. She leaned into me, and I suddenly felt protective. I had a strange urge to take care of her and see that she wasn't bullied by her mother. At half-time, she left to check with her friends. When she returned, she said, "Mom called. I feel like I'm being monitored."

I didn't sing out, "My mom's better than your mom," but I thought it. I'd been taught to respect my elders, but it goes both ways. It doesn't hurt for elders to return a little respect and some trust. Yet maybe her mother's suspicions were right on. Anyway, I wasn't going to back off. I liked being with Emily.

"Jason, I like you—a lot."

At that moment, I liked her a lot, too, all over, if you know what I mean. We were at the top of the bleachers. Nobody was watching, and I wouldn't have cared if they were. I kissed her, full on. I felt her hand on my neck pulling me to her. A feeling wrapped itself around me—and Emily felt it, too. I wanted it to last forever. People around us jumped up and yelled. They felt it, too, I thought. Wrong. Our team had just made the winning touchdown. Hathaway was taking home the Golden Pumpkin. I was almost dizzy, but it had nothing to do with the game.

"I've got to go. Mom will be waiting. I'll see you Monday."

"I understand, I think." I shook my head. "Do what you gotta do." Her friends were waiting for her at the bottom of the bleachers. They looked up at me and giggled.

Saturday morning, I lay in bed imagining Emily beside me, her hand on my neck. I had thought before about a moment like this, but without a face. Now, Emily was all I could think of. I couldn't let it go.

Mom knocked, then stuck her head in the door. "Jason! You're getting up this morning, aren't you? When the smell of pancakes and bacon doesn't bring you running into the kitchen, something's wrong. What's going on?"

"Does something have to be happening, just because a guy sleeps in?" Do all moms have radar?

"Not for everyone, but for you, yes. Sleeping in on a Saturday morning is not you. You wanna tell me about it, or are you keeping it to yourself?"

I said nothing.

"Then it has to be Emily. That must've been some ball game." At this, she smiled and gave me a look that meant "It's okay. Enjoy the moment," and she said, "Later on, we can talk about it if you feel like it. For now, get up and eat.

I topped off breakfast with a tall glass of OJ, grabbed my Broncos hat and my gloves, and headed for the garage. Saturday morning was my time to mow and edge the lawn and clean out the flower beds. My mind was not on lawn care. It's a wonder I didn't cut off a foot with the edger. As I followed the mower, I imagined Emily in the clutches of a domineering witch, unable to free herself, doomed to a life of servitude. A bit over-dramatic, but she might need a little help.

Mom and I had had talks about my growing up, being more independent, making more decisions for myself. I wished she could talk to Emily the same way, and even more to Mrs. Bradshaw. I thought Mrs. B had some growing up to do.

After school on Monday, while we waited for her mother to pick her up, Emily raised the subject. "I never really thought about it before. I can hardly make a move Mom's not a part of. I'd like to have a little room to breathe. I'm not sure she trusts me—or my judgment."

Mrs. Bradshaw stopped at the curb. She didn't look my way. Emily got in like a little puppy on an invisible leash, and they drove off. Maybe Mrs. B's problem was that she had a daughter. Don't mothers worry more about girls than boys? I knew a guy who got a girl pregnant when they were 18. It messed her up, and they both dropped out. I didn't want that. I would have a family someday, but not now. I had protection, and I knew how to use it. We'd gotten the banana-condom demo in every sex-ed class I ever took. However, feeling like I did about Emily, I could see how a guy could go a little crazy and lose control.

The next day, after we got settled at "our" table in the library, I put my hand on hers. I would have liked to do more, but not there. "I'm having a lot of trouble choosing a topic to write about." And I was going to keep on having trouble so long as it gave me an excuse to keep seeing Emily.

"You've already had some extensions. Monday is the last day you can turn it in before first-quarter grades come out, so you'd better get a move on," Emily said.

I finally decided to write about making higher education free for all. I thought of several reasons why that would be a benefit to everyone. Like someone said, spreading education was like adding a cup of water to the ocean. If you add enough, it lifts every boat in the world a little. Once I settled on the topic, the rest fell into place quickly. Emily took my paper home and returned it the next day. She liked it. Our English teacher read it and acted like I had changed from a worm to a butterfly.

───────────── ∽∾∿ ─────────────

I heard a knock on my bedroom door. Mom stuck her head in. "Jason, it's almost midnight. You never stay up this late on a school night. What's up?"

"Her mother doesn't think I'm good enough for her."

"Oh, really? Well, sometimes relationships work out, sometimes they don't. You learn to accept it and move on."

I didn't know how to tell my mother how strong my feelings were, or that I wasn't sure I was still in control of them. "How old were you when you started dating Dad?"

"I've told you before. I was sixteen. He was nineteen. Our families knew each other. Our first date was with two whole families. We went to a movie and took up most of a row in the theater."

"So how did you ever get together?"

"The first time was after a school bus trip to an away game. After we got back to Hathaway, your dad walked me home. On the way, we stopped in the darkness beneath a tree, and he kissed me. He said, 'I love you. I'll never do anything to hurt you.'"

<hr>

At the library, Emily phoned her mother and told her she was taking the bus home. Her mother said that was fine because she would be home late. When we got on the bus, we had to sit in seats facing each other. I couldn't keep my eyes off Emily. As soon as I could, I moved to sit beside her. My shoulder touched hers. That simple act aroused me. I laid my hand on hers and both our hands rested on her thigh. She jumped just a little.

The bus stopped. We grabbed our backpacks, got off, and stood there on the sidewalk, staring into each other's eyes. She made a slow turn and started toward her house, stopped, came back, and took my hand.

We sat on the lounge on her front porch. I had never been high or drunk, but I was pretty sure the feeling must be similar. I felt like the prow of a pirate ship headed into a storm, loving every moment of it. Was it worth it to get her in bed just to be doing it? I was having a hard time keeping my goal of getting laid in mind. I had this urge to be sure she was ready. I was losing focus. In that moment, I think I knew. I loved Emily.

She took my hands, drew me to my feet, and smiled.

It's a Grand Old Flag

J oy rippled across Levi Field as Darrell and I watched the San Francisco 49ers run in to take the Green Bay Packers. The scantily clad cheerleaders added a touch of enthusiasm, and both teams seemed eager to play. The flag was hoisted and we stood for the opening strains of the anthem, which always pulled at our heartstrings. I beamed as the 49ers stood erect in their red and gold uniforms—except—what's that? Two men sitting on their butts! Did my eyes deceive me? Was that Colin Kaepernick? Disrespecting the flag?

"What the hell?" I said. I *didn't fly halfway across the country for this!* I knew he couldn't hear me, but I yelled at the top of my voice, "Kaepernick! Get off your butt!"

Darrell said over the din, "Calm down. The newspapers said this might happen."

"What? You mean this was planned?"

The game continued, of course, but I couldn't get it off my mind. Back in the hotel, I said, "You knew what was going on?"

"If you ever read a paper, you'd know, too. Several players like Kaepernick have been sitting out the anthem. They say it's to protest the treatment of blacks in America."

"But why here?"

"Well, genius. If you protested, where would you get more attention—on a bus ride home, or in front of millions of viewers?"

"We spent a lot for tickets, the hotel, and plane fare to see the game—not to watch the flag being disrespected. I love the flag. Let them protest on their own time."

"Check the news. A lot of blacks are getting killed, and the police officers who shot them aren't punished. They get paid leaves—like a vacation."

"They're just doing their jobs, aren't they?"

"You've got to get out more. A lot of blacks are dying under questionable circumstances. People other than blacks are getting involved. It's like Boston Harbor. Remember the tea party? They were saying something's wrong. Politicians do it every election and even ask for our vote so they can fix what's wrong. Preachers tell us all the time we need change. Why shouldn't professional athletes have a voice?"

"If it was a protest, I guess it worked. The story's still on TV two weeks after the game."

On the bandwagon, Darrell continued, "You know, 'Black Lives Matter' does not imply white lives *don't* matter. The *real* message is: the life of a black person should not matter *less* than the life of a white person. What's wrong with protesting inequality?"

We were taught in school that if there is anything wrong, the person who calls attention to it is more of a patriot than those who keep silent. Perhaps Kaepernick is more patriotic than I am when all I do is stand and cheer. I finally see that our flag is not just a beautiful piece of material blowing in the wind. It stands for liberty and justice for all, equal liberty and equal justice.

Country

G imme a song that tells a story and touches my heart, a song about Mama makin' herself a dress out of flour sacks, and one for Rose to wear to school. Mama never got a day off, not even Sundays. Had supper ready for Daddy when he come home. A few times I saw him hug her in front of us. Whenever he took Mama dancin', we'd wait up as long as we could, hopin' to see them happy.

Daddy wanted to be a singer, had his guitar and all, and he could yodel good, made up a song about findin' the girl of his dreams. She had blue eyes and was from Texas. Mama told us she was the girl Daddy was singin' about. Daddy said the man singin' his song had on cowboy boots, a western shirt, a pistol at his side, and a Ranger's star on his chest, peace lovin' by nature. Daddy called his song "A Lotta Woman:"

Verse:
A smile on my lips
but not in my eyes.
Whisperin' sweet nothin's,
Nothin' but lies.
My eyes was wild
Till I met you,
And I give my heart
To your eyes of blue.

Chorus:
I swore to be true,
As true as I can,
'Cause you're a lotta woman
For just one man.

Verse:
I don't run around
From door to door.
My cheatin' heart
Don't cheat no more.
I never thought
I could be true.
But I'd be cheatin' myself
If I cheat on you.

Chorus:
I swore to be true,
As true as I can,
'Cause you're a lotta woman
For just one man.

There's Jimmy, he weren't right. We fretted, but we didn't know nothin' to do. When he got older, he was strong as a ox. Girls didn't want to be around him. Mama was scared he might get lost in the woods. She couldn't stand the thought of Jimmie out there all by hisself.

Me? Ain't much to tell. Walkin' two mile to school weren't no bother. Eight grades in one room. Rose was in second. Me and her walked together. Sometimes I give her a piggyback ride. When she fell asleep on her desk, Teacher let her sleep.

Teacher said I figured good. The world she told about were like a dream. Nothin' real about it to me. I just wanted to git home and have supper.

Lily was three. She wore only a diaper, 'cept in winter she had a coat.

We raised Blue from a pup, and his ears flopped like leaves on a tree. He slept most of the time, and he loved to hunt. Take out the squirrel rifle, and watch his eyes light up, sniffin', rarin' to go. When we lost Blue, I didn't cry. I bawled. Only time in my life. Did he run off? Someone musta stole him. I missed Blue somethin' awful.

Daddy went down to the mine. He never saw the sun 'cept a few hours on the Sabbath. He was a sad, sad man, and a mean drunk. Daddy's soul was black as the coal he brung up from the earth. If he stopped in a honkytonk on the way home, drownin' his sorrows in a few beers, look out. Mama waited up for him knowin' there'd be hell to pay.

The night he left, he come home and washed up. We ate supper and he sent us to bed. I heard him sayin' to Mama, "I'm sorry, but I gotta go. I gotta get outta here before I die."

"What about me and the kids?"

He said, "I'm sorry. Here's all I got," and he emptied his pockets on the bed. I could see him puttin' clothes in a sack.

"You're leavin' me and the kids without nothin'?"

He begun to cry but kept on packin'. "I'm a dead man if I stay. I gotta get out."

He put on his jacket, picked up his guitar, and went out the door. Watchin' out the window, I saw our old pickup drive away in the dark into the night, leavin' Mama with a hole in her heart.

I heard her prayin' and cryin' at the same time. I know'd she was on her knees by her bed. "Lord, what'll I do? What'll I do? Lord, he'p. You know the fix we're in." The springs squeaked when she got in bed. I thought she would never stop cryin'.

The preacher said he's prayin' for us, but he was as poor as us. People in the holler had their own to take care of. Jesus might help us, but I never saw him in our part of the county.

Mama scraped till her fingers was raw. She opened the cabinet doors, one by one. Ever' shelf was empty. She sold ever'thin' she could till we didn't have nothin' nobody wanted. But it weren't enough. We didn't know where to turn.

Three months after my daddy left, Floyd, the sheriff's assistant, deputy, or somethin', came sniffin' around. When he grinned his mouthful of teeth put me in mind of a possum.

The preacher told us about Satan temptin' Jesus. I thought Floyd was Satan, come to tempt Mama. We was hungry, and Floyd was, too. He set two sacks on the table and set down like he belonged. Mama looked at Floyd steady. She looked at Jimmie, and me, and Rose, and Lily. She looked at the groc'ries, and whispered, "I'll get supper." She did not smile.

Driving through the woods in my 4 x 4, I spotted the gray unpainted siding. Walking toward the house, it was hard to breathe. It was like I was carrying a heavy weight. My heart beat like a bass drum. Mama's gone, Jimmie's gone, Rose and Lily have families. I can't quit thinking how Mama cried the night Daddy left.

Travel Insurance

E velyn had anticipated a trip to Hawaii, but as the limousine drove away from the church, Matthew announced he had made reservations at the luxurious Ahwahnee Hotel in Yosemite National Park.

She said, "I thought we were going to the islands."

He said, "I wanted to surprise you. I've booked the honeymoon suite in the most beautiful place on earth. You'll love it."

Evelyn had always loved his enthusiasm and his manly way of taking charge, but his unilateral decision surprised her. She had packed her snorkel equipment and looked forward to sunning herself on the beach with an umbrella drink. Now they were off to the mountains.

They enjoyed Yosemite Falls, Bridalveil Fall, and Half Dome, as well as El Capitan, the granite monolith rising one half mile almost straight up from its base to its peak. Yet Matthew's decision, without consulting her, had placed a tiny burr in Evelyn's mind.

T he day after they returned from their honeymoon and Matthew left for his office, Evelyn called her best friend

Rosemary. "Let's do lunch," she said, and Rosemary jumped at the chance to hear about the honeymoon.

Evelyn asked the waiter to seat them in a quiet corner. "Rosemary, I hope you know how much I value our friendship. You've helped me over a lot of bumpy territory, and I appreciate it."

Rosemary gave a slight smile and a nod. "Thanks. What's this about 'bumpy territory?' The way you sounded on the telephone, I couldn't guess whether the news was good or bad. What happened in Hawaii?"

The waiter interrupted them to pour their tea, and they both ordered salads with vinaigrette dressing.

"So, good news or bad news?" Rosemary repeated.

"I'm not sure," Evelyn began. "It was a wonderful two weeks, but . . . "

"Go on," Rosemary said.

"I have no complaints about the honeymoon. We were waited on like royalty in the restaurant where Queen Elizabeth dined a few years ago. We picnicked by the river in the moonlight—but not in Hawaii." Evelyn told her about Matthew's honeymoon switch.

"You thought you were going to the islands. Instead, you had a good time at Yosemite." Rosemary shrugged. "What's the problem?"

"Last night, we were lying in bed. Then, out of nowhere, Matthew began talking about choosing a name for our first child."

"You're pregnant?" Rosemary gasped. "As long as we've been friends, I thought you'd tell me before you told Matthew."

I'm not pregnant," said Evelyn. "I don't need an anchor to drag around day and night for years. He's making assumptions as if I have no opinion."

"And he expects nothing more than a nod from you?"

"That's it in a nutshell."

"That's a side of him I never saw. Our dorm sisters would've been thrilled if the student body president had given them a glance, but you never know what's inside until you break the shell." She concluded, "Look, Evelyn. If a husband runs over his wife, he can only do it if she *lets* him."

Lunch came to a close with a final word from Rosemary. "All you have to do is stand up to him, and it ends there. Matthew controls his actions. You control yours. The sooner you realize that, the happier you'll be."

Evelyn thought about it but decided not to confront Matthew. *After all,* she thought, *he's the breadwinner. Perhaps that entitles him to a larger say in what we do.*

During the first two years of their marriage, Evelyn forgot about Matthew's earlier assumption that they would have children, until one night when they were watching the evening news on TV, and Matthew picked up where he left off as if it were yesterday. "If our first child is a boy, what name would you like?"

What? Evelyn thought. *We've still never had a serious discussion about having a family.* "Matthew, you've never asked me if I want to be a mother. You've gone past me, again, as if what I think doesn't matter."

"Oh, did I?" He seemed surprised but rushed on. "Well, eventually we should have a family. How about it?"

Evelyn recalled vague memories of her father. He was the decider, but his early death ended that. *At least,* she thought, *Matthew's not totally running over me.* But she never seemed to see it coming.

T en months later, identical twins Toby and Thomas were born. Their friends called Matthew and Evelyn "twice blessed."

Evelyn thought, *Twice is right—double the fun, and double the work. Two mouths to be fed at the same time, two bottoms needing diapers, and two little bodies with a temperature at the same time, with little or no support from Matthew.*

When the "Terrible Twos" hit, if there was mischief available, they got into it. If there was no mischief, they made it up. When one threw a temper tantrum, they both did. If one broke a toy, they fought over the one that remained.

Yet Evelyn enjoyed showing off her "Two T's" wherever she went. The minister cooed like a dove when he christened them. She dressed them in identical clothing, and while others had trouble telling them apart, she never did. Neither crawled in infancy, and both learned to walk on the same day. Matthew and Evelyn laughed aloud watching Toby and Thomas wriggling and waving their arms when music came on the television or radio.

On their first day in kindergarten, Evelyn shed a tear. Their blond curls and clear blue eyes charmed Miss Milam the minute they entered the classroom. They took to playing as seriously as if it were their first day of work.

When Evelyn returned home, the house was too quiet. The boys' bedroom was like an empty cavern. She wasn't sure she could stand it. *Call Rosemary,* she thought. She was reassured when she heard Rosemary's familiar laugh.

"I can feel it when you've hit a rough spot."

"You know me too well," Evelyn responded.

The waiter saw them coming. Without a word, he guided them to "their" table and opened menus for them. After they ordered, Rosemary said, "What's up now? I hope you're not pregnant again. You just got rid of the boys. I know—you love them. I also know you wouldn't want to take that job on again any time soon."

"Like, never, would be soon enough," said Evelyn. "But now that the boys are away at school, it's the silence I can't stand.

And Matthew? Sometimes I think he doesn't even know I'm alive." Her voice rising, she said, "I'm exhausted. The only thing Matthew has ever done at home is hire a gardener. He said if we ever sell, curb appeal adds a lot of value. I take care of the house, the bills, and the boys. I do all the shopping, cooking, and cleaning.

"Rosemary, will I ever listen to you? I know I'm the one who needs to change, but every time I decide to put my foot down, Matthew blindsides me, and we're off again, in a direction *he* chooses."

Rosemary said, "At least find a way to get out of the house. Volunteer. How about helping where the twins go to school? Schools usually welcome qualified help."

"That's a good idea. I can do that during the day, and Matthew won't object."

"Whether Matthew objects or not, diversify," Rosemary concluded.

When the twins were ready to leave elementary school, Evelyn was recognized at a school luncheon. "For help above and beyond the call of duty, John Muir Elementary School and staff want to thank and honor Evelyn," said the principal. "She began working a few hours a week in the office years ago. From there she moved into the classroom as an aide. Then she switched to Special Ed, serving students we know to be among the most vulnerable. Time and time again, she's earned the respect of administrators, teachers, and students. We thought about holding her boys back so we could keep her longer, but we feel sure she will be an asset wherever she goes."

Matthew was away at a convention.

When Toby and Thomas were in Middle School, Evelyn became indispensable to their teachers, like when their class decided to visit the Hershey's Chocolate Factory in Oakdale. Evelyn reserved the buses, arranged for sack lunches, enlisted parents to chaperone, and then double-checked everything.

The day after the field trip, when she and Rosemary got together for their "Lunchtime Therapy," Evelyn said, "Rosemary, I don't know how long you can tolerate my dumping on you, but Matthew did it again!" she said.

"Our trip ended with a picnic and games. He arrives right in the middle of the three-legged race. While the boys are still hopping along, Matthew parks the car and runs fast enough to meet them at the finish line. He grabs them in his arms and the cameras are snapping. Guess whose picture made the newspaper. You know, he's in every photo they ever took, smiling as if he had something to do with their successes."

"Look, I'm your best friend. I always will be. But let me be honest by asking, 'Where's your backbone?' You sound like a volcano ready to erupt, and I say, 'The sooner the better.'"

When the boys left for college, Matthew drove them to the university. "I'll get a chance to schmooze with the administration. Networking is the name of the game now," Matthew said.

Watching the car disappear around the corner, Evelyn felt an empty space in her heart. *Eighteen years of memories, too many to count,* she thought. *The boys' rooms, their empty closets—what should I do with them? Should I keep them for when they come home in the summer? The house is as quiet as a tomb.* She couldn't hold back the tears.

When Matthew returned from getting the boys settled in their dorm room, he burst into the house with a grin, rushing over to Evelyn to lift her off the floor in a bear hug. "News!" he said. "Your Matthew got a promotion with a huge raise a week ago. I'm the new manager of the Houston office."

"Houston? All our friends are here."

"The opportunity came at the perfect time. With the boys in college, we can start a new chapter. But that's not all. I want you to use your organizing skills. Be my office manager."

Evelyn's head was spinning. *Move? Office manager?* She was feeling desperate. "I'm off to visit Rosemary," she told Matthew. On the phone, she said, "Rosemary, I've got to see you before I go off the edge of the universe."

Seeing Evelyn so distraught, Rosemary said, "Calm down. You look awful. Are you sick? It's Matthew, again, isn't it?"

"He wants us to move to Houston, and he wants me to be his office manager. I'd be with him all day. I thought I would finally have some time for myself. Instead, he's planned my future as if I have no preferences—and I can't lose you as a friend!"

"I see," Rosemary said. "Until you stand up to Matthew, you'll never get off that train."

"So, what do I do now?" Evelyn said.

"Go, if you want, we'll still keep in touch, but you'll still have the same problem. You've got to tell Matthew how you feel. But please, look for a chance to escape. It might come when you least expect it," Rosemary counseled.

E velyn accompanied Matthew to Houston and organized his office so it hummed like a bee hive. She focused on the workplace atmosphere and treated employees with respect, and they repeatedly told her how much they enjoyed working for her. Two years in, she was caught off guard one day when Gregory, one of Matthew's partners, asked her out to lunch.

Over lunch, Gregory pointed out the skills she had demonstrated in the office. "I'm not here by accident," he said. "Your work here is just like my wife's. She works for the IRS and makes as much as I do. Have you thought about working for the government?"

"Me? Doing what? I don't even do our income tax reports."

"That's probably irrelevant. If you can make one office hum, you can do it anywhere. If you're as effective as you are here, in a year, you'll be bringing home as much as Matthew does."

Now, there's a thought. Could this be the escape hatch Rosemary foretold? The cage door was open, and out she flew. "Matthew, I'm turning in my badge."

Matthew had a blank expression, like a hunter whose favorite dog had just deserted him. "What do you mean?"

"I mean I've accepted a position with the IRS. I start in two weeks."

"What am I supposed to do?"

Evelyn looked him straight in the eye and without smiling said, "You'll figure it out."

Evelyn organized her corner of the IRS Center and began setting records for output. She molded her staff into a loyal team. Promotions came as quickly as regulations permitted.

———————————∞———————————

At Evelyn's retirement luncheon, she and Matthew sat on the right side of the Director of the IRS Center. In recognition of her 25 years of outstanding service, he said, "Evelyn is one rare individual. I can't describe how well she handled personnel, how she made all her staff feel appreciated, how she helped those who were struggling."

He went on to mention her computer skills, another factor in her rise to her executive position, and pointed out, "Most of the work in the entire building is data entry, a job that requires both skill and judgment. And during her tenure, Evelyn suggested changes in procedures that made their way into forms Americans now use when filing taxes. She climbed the executive ladder one rung at a time and retires as one of our top administrators at the Center."

As the speech and testimonials continued, Evelyn felt the curtain falling and thought, *Ye, gods! I'll be spending all day every day with Matthew.*

On the drive home, Matthew was silent. They parked and she unlocked the front door. Inside, his first words were, "Let's really celebrate. We could hire a band, have a dance, get some catered food, decorate the backyard with paper lanterns."

After 45 years of marriage, she thought, *we still can't agree on much of anything.* "I can't understand why your idea of celebrating is getting tipsy and dancing the night away. There must be a better way. Why not add another room to the house? We could both have a workroom or an office."

"A dance with friends here would be more fun than spending our nest egg on separate 'offices' where we won't see much of each other. How about a compromise—say a nice trip?" asked Matthew.

Evelyn thought, *Can it be that we might finally agree on something? A trip doesn't sound too bad. We could visit relatives out of state and renew family ties.*

But, Matthew, who didn't get along with her family, thought, *Cross the country in a small motor home and visit America's natural wonders. Take a cruise and see the world. We could visit all seven continents.*

Their conflicting ideas of a trip provoked a warmer-than-usual discussion. Evelyn gave in to "see the world," as Matthew put it. But she had a caveat: "If we travel, we're going to make it a real vacation."

"What do you mean 'a real vacation?'" Matthew challenged. "Haven't we always traveled in style?"

"Not really," she said. "You traveled in style. I handled all the arrangements. I bought tickets, made reservations, selected itineraries, reserved tours, and did the laundry and cooking. This time if we go, someone else will have to tackle the details."

"Hold that thought," Matthew pressed on. "Why not see a travel agent?"

M onday morning, he led her into the Moderne Travel Agency, "*First Class Trips, Our Specialty.*" Doris Doolittle greeted them with a blinding smile. She cooed, "Where would we like to go?"

"I'm thinking London, Paris, and Rome," Evelyn blurted out.

Matthew jumped in, "Or the Orient—China, India—or Australia."

Evelyn said, "That's too many third-world countries for me. I prefer places where I can wallow in luxury."

"Don't be a stick in the mud," said Matthew. "Let's get off the beaten path."

"Off the beaten path sounds like camping to me."

"Live a little, woman. We can see Europe in travelogues at the library and get a gut full of touristy places."

Evelyn's voice took on an edge. "You always do this. You finagle your own way, and I end up getting dragged to places I don't want to go and have no interest in."

"Our life is so hum-drum," Matthew pleaded. "How about seeing a part of the world that's strange to us? Be a little bit surprised?"

Evelyn seemed to relent. "What do you have in mind?" she offered.

"Malaysia," he answered quickly.

Evelyn coughed and turned red in the face, but not Doris. Her mind leaped into action. "A fascinating choice," she chanted, "from its ancient capital, Kuala Lumpur, to forests that have a greater biodiversity than almost any place in the world outside of the Amazon rainforest, of course."

Evelyn eyed Matthew. "I'm not going on a forced march through a jungle so you can see an exotic bird or a weird flower."

Ignoring her glare, Matthew said, "You agreed to go. Let's move on."

Doris, thinking of her commission, gently nudged. "Let me draw up plans. I'll have a package that will let you travel in comfort on tours that provide easy sightseeing. One last thing," she added. "Our trip insurance covers all contingencies: refunds for airfare and hotel accommodations, in case you have a change of plans, coverage in case of lost luggage, medical attention if you get sick—the works. We can insure any problem or destination you can imagine."

"How much does that add to the cost?" asked Matthew.

Doris, behind her sparkling fixed smile, was winding up her pitch. "We can add trip insurance for about 5% of your total package."

Matthew winced.

Evelyn had just passed the outer limits of her patience. "So, you *could* insure a trip to London? To Paris? To Rome?"

"Yes! Yes! Yes!" Doris was ecstatic.

"That settles it then. I'll take all three when I'm good and ready. Matthew, you go to Malaysia. Slog through the jungle, get eaten by mosquitoes, 'ooh' and 'aah' at strange birds and flowers—but count me out."

Matthew placed his hand on her arm. "Evelyn, don't be like that. Where would I go without you?"

When have you ever gone along with me? she thought. Smiling, she addressed Doris, "Could you provide insurance for a trip from here to home?"

Doris grinned and went along with the joke. "I think we could insure even a trip home."

"Well, that's where I'm going. As for you, Matthew—you can go to hell." Then, turning to Doris she asked. "Can you insure a trip like that?"

Amber, the Giant Slayer

Y ou might be familiar with the story of David and Goliath when a young soldier killed a nine-foot-tall giant and sent the Philistine army running in fear. Just as dramatic is the story of my granddaughter, a middle-aged single parent, and an automotive Goliath. The story follows.

―――――――――――――⌘―――――――――――――

A n unlicensed, underaged, uninsured driver totaled Amber's Ford. The impact from the airbag and seatbelt injured her breast, bruised her legs and abdomen, and gave her a black eye. In a flash, she had lost the best car she had ever owned, had no way to continue her three jobs, and feared her insurance rates might go up even though she was not at fault.

It took three weeks for the insurance company to send her a $9,000 check for the loss of her car—a check she expected to use as a down payment on a new car. In the meantime, without transportation, she had to scrape up money for food delivery and pay for rides when she went out.

Researching online, Amber was surprised to find a new vehicle on a dealer website listed at $19,500 that might be in her price range if she could arrange affordable payments. She told the dealer how much she had to put down.

Years earlier, shopping for her now-wrecked Ford, Amber told the salesperson the car she wanted, how much she would pay per month, and for how long. The salesperson tried to move her in another direction, but she did not waver even a half percentage point. Finally, when it seemed negotiations were at a stalemate, and she told him she would look elsewhere, he looked apoplectic, made a dash for his head office, and returned quickly to say she could have the car on her terms.

So, before making a trip to the car lot, she wanted this dealer's assurance she wouldn't get the runaround.

He promised her he could get close to what she requested, so her friend in Fresno drove 40 miles to Visalia to pick her up; then they drove to a neighboring town to the dealership.

She test-drove the car and filled out an application for financing. Their finance handler came to the salesperson's office and said the monthly payments would be $400. Amber expressed alarm because she had told the salesperson before driving there, she could only handle about $180.

The finance man said, "What do you expect, buying a vehicle that costs over $27,000?"

She showed him a screenshot of their website showing the price of $19,500 and the VIN—the same as the car she test-drove.

Years ago, Amber began her career in management at a music store where she had customers returning to deal specifically with her. They trusted her because she knew what they wanted, how much the store paid for it, and how much she could discount the product, still making money while satisfying the customer. In other words, she understood the game that goes on between salespeople and customers.

So, she waited patiently while the salesperson and finance man went to another room and returned shortly, saying she could have the new vehicle with payments of $250 a month, but they still tried to persuade her to buy a used car instead.

She became visibly upset, shouting a few unprintable words for the benefit of clients and employees in neighboring offices, and returned home to calm down and search for another vehicle.

L ater that evening, during dinner at her friend's house, the salesperson phoned. He had figured out how she could get the vehicle for the price she was willing to pay. The deal he offered was $9,000 down with monthly payments of $209.

She accepted his offer. He assured her he would arrange the financing but told her he had to get it approved. They played phone tag for three days, leaving Amber uncertain she would get the car. When he finally got back to her on Saturday and she reminded him of the deal they had agreed on, he said she was confused, and he told her about a deal they had not discussed for more money than they originally agreed on, a ploy she called gaslighting. He acted like he had no memory of their previous conversation. When she insisted, he transferred her to his manager, who tried to force a different deal on her.

That's when Amber hit social media, posting reviews of her experience on Google and Yelp. She also went to the manufacturer's website and filed a complaint detailing her experience at the dealership. Soon after she posted reviews, the manager called and attempted to push her into yet a different deal, insisting that it was the best he could do. She held her ground.

Then, five minutes later, the same man called, telling her he would honor the deal she asked for on her first visit. He asked in return that she remove her reviews from the Internet. In good faith, she did.

Suddenly, after showing no concern for wasting her time and resources, they were in a hurry to finish the deal right away. She told them she did not have a ride to their dealership, plus her bank was closed until Monday. They threatened the car might be sold to someone else over the weekend and said they could not hold the vehicle. When she threatened to repost her reviews, they reluctantly agreed to hold the car over the weekend.

On Monday, Amber made her down payment, dropped her case against the dealership, and drove away victorious in an excellently priced new car.

The Curve

Residents along the dirt road scurried out of its path when the monstrous vehicle roared down the lane, raising clouds of dust and hurling clods of rain-soaked earth. The truck turned into the drive of the largest house on the block, and a middle-aged man emerged from the driver's side.

Across the street from the man's Victorian-style mansion, a new resident of a flagstone house, a blonde with a ponytail, knelt in her parking strip, planting a tree. The man strode across the street, and without introduction said, "The cottonwoods you're planting will be a pain later when they start shedding all over the neighborhood."

She ignored the man and continued planting her cottonwood tree. He was miffed. He stalked away, thinking, *I'll have to find a way to put that little lady in her place.*

A few days later, the woman with the ponytail drove home a new, silver sedan with a unique feature in its rear axle. She could drive at an unusually high speed around the curved embankment that led from their street onto the roadway into town.

When the man noticed her taking the curve, he bought a stopwatch. The same day, stopwatch in hand, he approached the curve in his SUV. His pulse heightened as he clicked the stem, setting the watch in motion. The needle swept around the face of the watch as he completed the curve. Then he snapped the stem to check his time. With each trip around the corner, he kept trying to improve, if only by a fraction of a second.

The points he chose for timing himself were so obvious he could also time her car, her new car, as she took the same curve.

One day, the blond with the ponytail was at the corner where the street curved, having coffee with a neighbor. As the SUV drove past, she observed the driver's left hand in the air, holding something—what, she wasn't sure. When he rounded the curve, his hand pumped.

She said to her neighbor, "I believe our neighbor is timing himself. Could he be jealous at how fast my car takes the corner?" *What a putz,* she thought. *First, he tries to tell me what tree to plant. Now, he wants to race. Well, if that's what he wants, bring it on. He can be number one, but only if he can beat me.*

On her way into town later, she rounded the curve at a daring, even reckless speed. Without looking or even seeing the man, she knew he was timing her. Later in the day, she stared as his vehicle took the curve as if it had suddenly become his enemy.

The woman began having coffee with her neighbor each morning to observe his expression. When she succeeded in besting him, he looked tortured. But once he trumped her, even slightly, he smirked like a bully who had taken over a playground. His smugness provoked her to go even faster the next time, forcing him back into his melancholy.

She studied the curve like a professional racecar driver, practicing the exact moment when to hug the inside and when to accelerate. A few days later, seeing him in his driveway, she gunned her motor. In her rearview mirror, she saw him reach into his pocket. The watch was surely coming out. Her engine growled as she backed out. Moving quickly to high gear, she rushed headlong toward the turn.

Nearing the corner, her ponytail bounced as she jammed the accelerator to the floor. Her car dived for the inside of the curve, caroming into the outer edge. Her tires gripped the road like tigers' claws. Euphoria swept over her as she straightened out on the opposite side. In a few minutes, she returned to the driveway and sat there breathless for a few minutes.

Back inside, standing in her kitchen, she heard a roar from across the street. He burned rubber as he zoomed toward the curve.

As he shot past, she thought, *I'll give it to him. He's got guts, to take it at that speed.*

The second she saw him enter the curve, she gasped. His front wheels leaped over the top of the arch. His SUV shot into the air like a plane taking off. It soared over the embankment, and floated for a second like an iron blimp, landing with a thud—right side up in an open field.

For an instant, she was concerned he might have hurt himself. She thought about getting in her car and driving to the corner to check on him. Then she heard his wheels zinging, trying to get traction. When she saw his vehicle over the berm, she retreated to the inner sanctum of her house to watch from her window.

He drove past her into his driveway, got out of his car, and placed an object under the rear tire. Then he got back into his car, closed the door, and carefully and deliberately backed over his stopwatch.

Crazy Joe

The following story was passed down to me
by my grandfather, Luther Williams,
who was born in Tennessee in 1845,
fought in the Civil War,
and lived in Mississippi, Missouri,
Oklahoma Territory, Oklahoma,
Old Mexico (now New Mexico), and Texas.

D oes every small town in Texas have some old man who tells tales so fantastic people think he's a liar, a lunatic, or, possibly, telling the truth? The answer is a resounding yes.

People weren't always sure what my grandfather's real name was, but they sure remembered his amazing stories, which attested to the many jobs he had, none of them highly technical but all requiring some skill.

He had rough-necked in the oil fields where he helped bring in some of the greatest gushers in west Texas. He worked down in the Gulf on a fishing boat for about three years. Sure, fishing's a leisurely life after the lines are prepared—that is, until you strike a run of fish. Then it's pure hard work till you're too tired to lift your pole.

My grandfather was a cowboy, and anyone who knows about the real west knows that being a cowboy requires many skills, including the skill and the will to survive. He could preach a little fire and brimstone, too, and he never failed to take up a collection. One Sunday, he began a whopper of a tale.

———————— ⨯⨯⨯ ————————

A s quickly as my Grandpa began his story about seeing a cowboy jump from the top of one mountain to the top of another, he met a solid wall of skepticism. Texans knew about flash floods that swept everything in their path and changed the landscape. They also knew Texas had hills, but no mountains. Even so, the way Grandpa described it, there were two mountains, side by side. A mighty storm brought heavy rains creating a rushing stream between them, washing away the soil at the base of each. The mountains began tilting towards one another. As the base continued to wash away, the mountains moved ever closer.

When the rain stopped, the cowboys gazed in wonder at the two mountain peaks, once far apart, now remarkably close. The sparse soil underneath those two points gave no guarantee of support for the two arms jutting out towards each other like long bony fingers.

But "Crazy Joe," whose nickname had always bothered him, declared he could jump across the chasm from one mountaintop to the other. If he succeeded, no one would ever call him "Crazy Joe" again. Maybe they'd change it to "Hoppin' Joe," or "Jumpin' Joe," or some such other title. Anything besides "Crazy."

The gap was not enormous, but neither was it small. Crazy Joe would have to get a good run to make the distance, but he was known to win footraces. The cowboys began placing bets. Those who bet against Crazy Joe figured the distance between the two points was not impossible, but the ground had been soaked by the rains, and the two peaks could collapse at any moment, preventing Crazy Joe from reaching his destination. The other side agreed it was risky, but argued if Crazy Joe made it, they would double their money, and if he missed, they wouldn't lose much.

Crazy Joe had no idea how long the opportunity to change his name would present itself, so he told the cowboys he'd make the jump the following morning at daybreak.

I n the early dawn, the men drank strong, dark coffee around a campfire. Soon after sunrise, they gathered on the side of the gap along with Crazy Joe. His eyes were bugging out, and he rolled them like two shiny marbles. A path was cleared for him, and he walked it a couple of times to be sure no loose sticks or stones might impede his progress. Giving it his approval, he walked back from the gap about 25 or 30 paces.

He got rid of all the extra weight he could: his pistol and belt, his Double D Stetson (revealing hair that had not seen soap or a comb for a while), and even his shirt. He kept his hand-tooled boots. Like any good cowboy, if he didn't make it, he wanted to die with his boots on, not to mention the fact that the ground was rocky and uneven. He crouched down like he was in a race—which he was—a race against time and space.

The men shouted, "Crazy Joe. Like a bird! Like a bird! Like a bird!" The chant transfixed him. He could fly—like a bird!

As he began to run and picked up speed, the chanting faded into wide-eyed apprehension. They might never see Crazy Joe alive again. He dashed between the lines of men and flung himself into mid-air. He sailed like a fledgling on his first trip out of the nest, arcing first up, his legs flailing in space, then down. As he landed on the other side, a cheer went up. He made it! He would no longer be Crazy Joe.

He lit flat-footed on the other point and spun around, with one hand raised in the air like he was square dancing, acknowledging the cheers. Grandpa looked down to retrieve the money bag holding the bets when he heard a resounding crack. It wasn't quite like an earthquake, but clearly, something had broken or moved. The top of the mountain where Crazy Joe landed gave way under his weight. The cowboys watched as Crazy Joe threw up his hands in a helpless gesture and disappeared without a cry into the chasm below.

--- ∞ ---

My grandfather announced, "He made it," and divided the money among those who bet he would, and everyone got off the mountain quick.

But, what do you know? About two months later, Grandpa was up about 20 miles east of McKinney, Texas, near the Red River. It was the fourth Sunday, and the preacher hadn't shown up. They waited a respectable time, then went on with the service. After some gospel singing, Grandpa rose to bring a message. It was still March, but close to Easter, so he chose the text: "Though he were dead, yet shall he live."

He was just getting warmed up when he spied a man a few rows back whose face looked familiar, but he couldn't place him. The man was scratched up as if he had recently fought a bear. Suddenly, he knew! Dagnabit! It was Crazy Joe! Grandpa interrupted his sermon and exclaimed, "Crazy Joe! You're alive?"

"Yep," he said, "it's me."

Grandpa told the folks to sit down and get ready to hear a story like they probably never heard before. He told them what he knew, up to the part where Crazy Joe disappeared. Then he said, "We all saw you go down. What happened, Crazy Joe?"

And Crazy Joe was happy to oblige. He said, "Well, just after I landed on the other side, I heard a loud snap. There was nothin' I could do. I was goin' down for sure. All I could do was shout, 'God, save me!' The dirt beat me to the bottom by a second or two. It was just mud, deep mud. I was in it, almost to my chest.

"It took me all day to get shed of the mud and dig my boots out. It was 'most dark when I started walkin'. I was feared I might freeze to death. When I got up on a small rise, I spotted a light a good piece away. I walked till I was all tuckered out. I thought I was gonna die more than once. Then the light I seen went out, but I kept on going. When I got there, it was just a little shack. At the door, I hollered loud as I could to raise someone. After a while, a light come on.

"A voice shouted, 'I got a loaded shotgun aimed at the door. What do you want? Who are you?'

"That's the last thing I remember because I went down like a rock. When I come to, they told me they waited a while, then they come out to see about me. They drug me inside, washed me off, and put me to bed. They put salve and liniment on my scrapes and kept watch on me.

"Soon as I felt well enough, I pitched in to split some wood and done some fence-mendin', to pay 'em back a little. Today's the first chance I got to go to church. I wanted to be in the Lord's house on the Lord's day, seein' as how He saved me like He did."

Grandpa declared, "This is Crazy Joe's testimony."

Folks sat hypnotized till one deacon stood up and said, "Praise the Lord!" They all nodded in agreement.

Grandpa said, "Amen. Let's eat and rejoice."

People spread out their lunches, incredulous. Some laid out blankets on a few grassy spots; some picnicked in their wagons; some ate standin' up, talkin' on and on about Crazy Joe.

I was sure we'd never hear another story to match that one.

Bump

The print was small, so Stan urged, "Mama, go faster so I can read it."

"I can't get close enough for you to read that," she replied. "It wouldn't be safe." But when they came to a red light, he pressed her to move closer, and she did. The bumper sticker read:

**If you can read this
you're too close**

Stan smiled. Bumper stickers made being in the car more fun. The first bumper sticker Stan stuck on the VW van his mother bought him said simply:

49ers

He knew all their stats and was loyal even when they were in a slump. He placed the red and gold decal in the center of the rear bumper. It was soon joined by a second sticker, a takeoff on the name of Jesus—shaped like a fish but with legs. It said:

Darwin

Stan attached his second bumper sticker along the bottom of the driver's side below the door and began parking on the far side of the double driveway to avoid his mother's eyes. This one read:

SHIT HAPPENS

He had never seen a bumper sticker that said:

GRACE HAPPENS

. . . and if he had, he wouldn't have put it on his VW. That wasn't life as Stan saw it. Years after dropping out of school, Stan still lived at home with his mother. He would move out tomorrow if he could afford it.

Eventually, Stan's car was trimmed with stickers arching over the wheel wells from front to back on both sides and above the windows. He gained some notoriety when a newspaper reporter did a feature about him and his sticker fetish.

To make the shot more interesting, the photographer said, "Get in the car and hang out the window." In the picture, Stan's upper body stuck out of the window while his left hand was making a peace sign. The wind had lifted his long hair off his neck and his grin showed a perfect set of teeth. Neighbors who saw the picture and read the story had already given him a nickname, *Bump*. His best friend Dave teased that he was about as useful as *a bump on a log*.

F rom his room, Stan could hear his mother trudging down the hall with her sample cases. The cosmetics were heavy, so he went to help her. He arranged the cases in the back of her SUV, and she came out carrying an umbrella. It might rain.

The phone rang and Stan rushed to check the caller ID before his mother got to it. When he saw who was calling, he let it ring. "Who's that on the phone?" his mother yelled.

He didn't answer. Instead, he said, "I'm going over to Dave's to hang out till he goes to work." He got in his van and left before she did.

Dave, in pajamas and with bare feet, answered Stan's knock at the door. His hair was mussed; it always was. It had a weird natural wave so that whether it was long or short, combed or not, it looked messed up. His boss at *Jack-in-the-Box* made him wear a hairnet from the time he came in the door until the time he checked out.

"Hey, man," said Dave, "where's the fire?" as he went to the kitchen to start the coffee.

Finding out Dave's mother was at work, Stan spoke freely. "I think I've got a job lined up. I'm not sure, but it looks good. Mother will explode when she hears what it is."

"Explode? What is it? Robbing banks?" He could not suppress a smile.

"It's reading tarot cards for people over the phone—working for a psychic hotline."

"You're kidding. They'll pay you to do that?"

"It's part-time, $12.50 an hour. My problem is that I need a phone line. I'll have to ask mom for help. I don't know how much it will cost, but when it's up and running, I'll be raking in the dough."

Dave poured coffee for them. "I'm not like you. You know my brain won't work without a caffeine jump start." He took a sip. "Now, what were you saying?"

Stan said, "Just think. We could move out and share an apartment like we've always talked about."

"Apartments are expensive. Just paying half the rent would be a stretch for me. Every time I work up to asking my manager for a raise, they change managers. I'm still stuck at minimum."

"Let's wait and see how much I bring in."

They talked all day till it was time for Dave to go to work. "I hear Jack calling, 'Come flip my burger.'"

W hen Stan arrived home, the house was empty and silent. He was used to that. He made himself a baloney sandwich. His mother bought good baloney. He liked it with Jack cheese and lots of mayonnaise. With a glass of iced tea, he had just sat down to eat when he heard his mother's SUV pull up and the motor stop. He sat at the kitchen table and waited, hearing her drop her sample cases in the spare room.

After a hard day pushing cosmetics, she was tired. The minute she spied him in the kitchen she began. "Did you look for a job today? Did you even apply? You can't live like this forever. I'm going to die someday, you know." It was like a mantra. Her eyes looked tired, but she mustered up the energy to say, "You're a nice boy. If you'd get a haircut and show as much interest in getting a job as you do in bumper stickers, you might get someplace in life."

He was keenly aware that by her estimate, he had not gotten anywhere in life. Stan had worked several jobs since high school. He laid carpet long enough to get pretty skilled, and had carried heavy rolls of carpet and padding, alone when necessary. His knee still hurt from using the kicker to tighten carpets at the edges. He might still be doing it, but when he tried to make a few suggestions to his boss, a few too many his mother suspected, they let him go without notice. He was glad enough. He might have injured his knee permanently.

He washed dishes in a high-class restaurant, but they wanted slave labor for minimum wage. The restaurant catered to a classy clientele, but there was nothing Stan saw in the kitchen that was high class. There wasn't enough ventilation to keep the air healthy, and the large vats he cleaned with caustic substances might have affected his lungs. Stan wasn't going to kill himself for what they paid. He had tried other jobs, but none of them had lasted. *Bad luck*, he thought.

He waited for his mother to pause for a breath, and then said, "As a matter of fact, I got a job today."

She spun around like she had won the lottery. "You did? What is it? When do you start?" Then her eyes narrowed. "Exactly what job did you get?"

"I'll be making $12.50 an hour working part-time. I figure at $12.50 an hour, minus taxes, I should clear about $1,700 a month. That's over $20,000 a year. I could get an apartment, and even start paying you back. That's more money than any of the other jobs I've had." He hoped his reference to moving out would soften the impact of his answer to her question.

"What's the job?" she repeated.

"Reading tarot cards."

"Oh, my God!" she said. "Another hair-brained scheme."

"I got a job reading cards for a psychic network."

She was still shaking her head.

"Hear me out. All I need is a phone to take calls. I can work here at home. You'll have to help me with a new phone line, but I'll pay you back out of my first check."

"Tarot cards? What do you know about tarot cards? Is that the scam of the month?"

"Let me explain," Stan calmed her. "I've been reading cards for years. My friends say I'm pretty good. I'm usually right about their problems."

She was still trying to take it all in. "How on earth did you ever find a job like that?"

"I saw an ad in the newspaper for a part-time reader. It said: 'Wanted: card readers: $12.50 an hour, 25 hours a week part-time,' and gave a phone number. I couldn't sleep for a whole week thinking about it, so I called."

She stared directly at Stan but did not move.

"Their machine said to leave a name, number, and a message about your experience, and to say if you're calling for a trainee position. The next day, Heidi, a coach from the

Psychic Power Line called. She gave me a time to call back and give her a sample reading."

With a sigh, his mother folded her arms under her breasts and her lips tightened like a child refusing to take medicine.

"The next day I did a reading for the coach. She explained the job and said I'd be working from home. I got a contract in the mail that said I would be giving 'massages' over the phone." He laughed at the typo. "I think they meant messages. I thought it was cool, so I signed it." He added, "But I need a phone."

"And you expect me to pay for it? Do you know how much a new phone line costs? If this doesn't last any longer than other jobs you've had, that's money down the drain. Can't you find something better?"

"You're always bugging me about getting a job, so at least let me try it. We'll never know if I can do this unless you help me." Stan was sliding home. "Maybe this is a chance to get me out of your hair." He grinned. He knew she would say yes.

"Okay. I give up. I'll do it," she said, "on one condition. We get a speakerphone. As long as I'm paying the bill, I'm entitled to know what I'm paying for." She shook her head and mumbled as she turned to leave, "I must be crazy."

Stan remembered his bumper sticker:

GOOD VIBRATIONS

The technician from the telephone company installed the new line three days later. Stan bought a white Slimline phone with caller ID and a callback feature, in case he needed it—and a speakerphone. It sat on a small table by his bed. As quickly as the lineman left, Stan dialed the psychic hotline to give them his number.

They said, "Now it's only a matter of time. You can sign in this afternoon, then wait for your first caller. Good luck, Stan."

A t 9:00 P.M. he picked up his phone and logged in. A recorded voice went on for several minutes, a generic speech to all readers. "What a marvelous job you're doing! Thousands of people have been logging on, and we expect to be busier tonight than ever before. Go get 'em, team!"

Stan hung up and sat on his bed waiting. He could see his mother across the hall, watching TV, listening for the sound of the phone. Five minutes passed before the phone rang.

Stan picked up the receiver and recorded the time. "Good evening. Welcome to PPL. How're you doing?" His mother walked in and sat in the only chair in the room, her hands in her lap.

A female voice asked, "Is this part of my five free minutes?"

"Yes. My name is Stan, and my extension is 40667, in case we get cut off. May I please have your name, and will you spell it?"

"Melissa Perls, P-e-r-l-s."

"And Melissa, when is your birthday?"

"December 24."

"And the city you're calling from?"

"Charlotte, North Carolina."

"How ya doin', Melissa?"

She didn't seem to know how to proceed, so Stan said, "I'm a card reader. Do you have a question for me?"

"Yes," she said. "I don't quite know how to put this."

He guessed. "Is it a marital problem, Melissa?"

"How did you know?"

"I must be a bit psychic." They both laughed.

"Melissa, here's what I want you to do for me: Close your eyes and concentrate on your problem. I'll begin shuffling the cards. When you have the problem clearly in mind, you say stop." He began to shuffle, and she stopped him during his third round.

"Okay, now I'm going to cut the deck into three stacks. You choose which stack you want me to use for your reading."

She chose the second stack, and he said, "Just give me a few seconds to lay out the cards, and we'll begin."

His mother watched as he placed the cards on his bedside table in a clock-like pattern, the first two in the center, and two each at 6:00, 9:00, 12:00, and 3:00. The remaining eight cards went two each at 4:30, 7:30, 10:30, and 1:30. It was important they were dealt in that exact order. Stan had discovered from experience that changing the order fouled up the messages he picked up from the cards.

Melissa interrupted. "I think my five minutes are up. I have your extension. I'll call you right back."

The phone went dead, and he recorded the time: 9:11. He was sorry he had spent so much time shuffling and dealing, but he couldn't vary from his procedure.

With brows furrowed, Stan's mother looked skeptical. "Do people actually believe they can find out anything important about their lives from a stack of cards?"

———— ∞ ————

S tan fidgeted with his pencil and notepad, but he didn't touch the card layout. The phone rang. It was Melissa.

"I wasn't sure I was going to get through to you. I had to dial twice."

"Well, Melissa, I guess you're just lucky." Stan was moving into familiar territory. He began his reading by turning over the two cards in the center. "Melissa, I see the Fool and the King of Wands inverted, and I'm seeing something that looks like you're at a crossroads with your marriage. Something's happened to give you doubts about the relationship. It appears that you and your husband are not fighting, but it looks like you're more friends than husband and wife. Is that correct?"

"That's pretty close," she replied. Stan glanced at his mother who shook her head.

Stan looked at the cards at the 6:00 position, the King of Cups inverted and the Devil. "I see another man trying to enter the scene. Is that correct?"

"You're right," she said. "You're amazing."

"This other man looks like maybe an ex-husband. He's still interested in you but only physically, not so much for who you are." At the 3:00 position, he turned over the Five of Wands and the Ace of Discs. "I'm also seeing that there's a trip that's in question? Are you wondering if you should go?"

"You nailed it! I just separated on peaceful terms from my husband after seven years. We thought our marriage was going nowhere. We're still talking, and we have no children to consider—neither of us wanted any. Now my 'Ex' has called, asking me to go with him to a cabin in the mountains for the weekend."

"Why do you think he's suddenly interested in you?"

"While we were married, I got a little on the heavy side, but since divorcing him, I've been working out. I ran into him in the supermarket. He didn't recognize me till I tapped him on the shoulder. He said he couldn't believe how gorgeous I was."

Stan knew that he had the option to stop reading the cards and simply discuss her problem, but he believed the cards. He had read cards many times, and every time he did, he found some reason, great or small, to reaffirm his faith in them.

Stan picked up the cards at the 4:30 position—the Queen of Wands and the Lovers inverted. "He's only interested in you because of your good looks. He doesn't want to get married; he just wants the honeymoon."

Stan's mother left the room. It was time for her nightly bowl of vanilla ice cream with Hershey's chocolate topping. When she returned a few minutes later, ice cream in hand, Stan was still talking to the same person, and they were still on the same topic.

Melissa said, "He's invited two friends for the same weekend, and I'm not sure if they'll bring girls with them. I don't always get along with other women."

The cards in the 10:30 position were the Nine of Swords and the Ten of Swords. "Melissa, I'm going to be completely honest about what I see in the cards."

"Please," she said, "be honest. Don't hold back."

He warned, "There are signs that there could be an element of danger in the trip. It might be a good idea to find out if there will be other women present."

"I trust my ex-husband. I've never had reason to mistrust him."

"Still," Stan said, "the cards indicate an element of danger. Don't totally ignore that possibility."

"Oh! I've been on longer than I should've. This might break my bank, but thanks for the reading, and most of all, thanks for being upfront with me."

The call lasted 60 minutes. "Boy!" Stan said putting the phone down. "Is she going to be mad when she gets the bill! At $3.99 a minute, that'll add up big time."

"Doesn't she know she could see a therapist for a lot less money?" Stan's mother blurted out. "I can't believe she told you all those private things. What sort of people take advice from fortune tellers about their personal lives?"

Stan was not deterred. "I've done this a lot of times with friends. I thought I had to be face to face to do a reading, but I guess not. This is the first time I've tried it on the phone."

He thought, *"I've finally found something I like to do, and I'm making money at the same time."* He had a bumper sticker that said:

No Fear

At the end of his first week, Stan got a call from Heidi, his psychic line coach. "Hey, Stan." Her voice had a smile in it. "You've logged a lot of time in your first week with PPL. You're great. I'm just calling to point out something you need to remember. You got a lot of calls, but most of them were short. Remember, we average your minutes by the number of calls. If you have a high average, our machine automatically sends you more calls. If your average is low, you don't get as high a priority."

"I understand," he said—and he did. The longer people are on, the more money the company makes.

Heidi continued, "With free minutes for first-time callers, we actually go in the hole on short calls. We want you to give people answers to their questions, but remember, every minute you keep them on helps your average." She laughed. "Maybe you could just give them their answers a little more slowly."

"I'm not sure I can do that. Sometimes the question is simple, and I can find an answer for them in a few minutes."

"That's true, of course, but callers like friendly readers. Sometimes they just hang around to chat for a while. If they like you, they'll call back and ask for your extension. At PPL we call that 'filling your stable.'"

Stan understood the term. His mother had a "stable" of cosmetic clients. He guessed she kissed a lot of ass to sell as much as she did, but that wasn't for him. Dealing with people's lives was serious, not a scam.

He got a call toward the end of his second week. "Whatever you're doing must be right, Stan. Your average has gone way up. Keep up the good work. You're on the priority list. You should be getting a stream of calls."

And Heidi was right. The calls came thick and heavy.

S tan logged in each night about the time his mother's favorite TV shows came on. She liked Jessica Fletcher and Andy Griffith. She didn't like shows with a lot of sex and violence. The door to Stan's room stayed open, but she tried to keep the sound down.

One night, walking past his door, Stan's mother stopped. He had a call from a man in the military stationed in Hawaii. When she heard the caller say that he was having sex with a married man, an officer who was still in the closet, she stifled a little gasp.

"When we're together, we're really intense," the caller said. "We really hit it off. Physically, we really communicated well for a month or more, then he stopped taking my calls. I know he's busy, but I guess it was just an affair, and he'll never call again." With that, Stan's mother walked out of the room and closed the door behind her.

Stan told the man to wait while he shuffled and laid out the cards. He reasoned that cards don't care if people are straight or queer.

He turned over the first two cards and began. "It might be you'll never hear from your officer friend again, but the cards indicate you're going to run into each other. There's a social function that I see you'll be attending."

"That's true," he said. "He and his wife will be there."

"Play it cool," Stan said. "Act as if nothing has happened, and let nature take its course."

W hen Stan's first paycheck came in the mail, he was so excited that he just held the envelope in his hand for a while. In his mind, he could see his dreams coming true. He could be his own person and no longer an appendage of his mother. This was the first big step on his stairway to freedom. However, when he saw the amount, it looked more like half a step. He called Heidi.

She explained, "There are deductions—and the checks are always a week behind real time. Remember, you're being paid by the minute. The in-between minutes are on your own time."

Still, his check was large enough so Stan could say, "Hey, mom, here's $75 for the phone line and a little rent." He treated Dave to a meal at a place where people ordered off a menu rather than looking at a wall. Stan wished he had a bumper sticker that read:

Stan of Haskel Drive is Employed

The next day Stan and Dave went apartment hunting. The manager in a large complex ushered them into just what Stan had in mind: a two-bedroom, two-bath apartment that had a large living space. When she told them the rent, they glanced at each other in disbelief.

"You have to pay your first and last month's rent, plus a cleaning deposit which you get back if the apartment is in good shape when you leave. We pay for cable, water, and garbage. You pay for your electricity and phone."

They thanked her and retreated to Stan's car. "Wow!" said Dave. "If we get an apartment, it's not going to be here!"

Stan said, "I never realized how much cash it takes upfront to get into an apartment. The deposit, first and last month, telephone, utilities, plus furniture. I'm way short." His eyes twinkled as he turned to Dave. "Why don't we ask the cards?"

He would have read the cards right then, but the only time Stan had read for Dave, it scared the shit out of Dave. He had told Dave, "I see that you've seen someone recently about a health-related sexual problem, and he told you not to worry. Is there anything you want to tell me?" Dave had blushed.

Then, Stan revealed the rest of Dave's fortune. "I see some danger coming into your life very soon, but it won't be fatal."

On his way home, Dave was broadsided by a girl driving a Dodge Neon. She went to the hospital, but Dave walked away from it. After that incident, whenever Stan offered to read for him, Dave declined. "The only future I want to know is if I'm going to win the lottery!"

Dave was not hopeful. "Jack pays minimum, and only 10 cents extra for swing shift."

"But at least, it's steady," said Stan. "Imagine being free of our parents. We could invite a couple of ladies over, barbeque on the patio, and do what comes naturally." He felt like a bird perched in the open door of a cage. The thought of flying free excited him. Stan had a bumper sticker from "In-N-Out Burger," and as many others had done, he removed the "B" and the "r" off Burger before he stuck it on his VW.

In-N-Out urge

Stan needed money, lots of it, so for the next month he worked long shifts as many days as he could, keeping a careful record of his minutes, but by the time he had talked off and on for hours, his brain felt like it had been pureed and his body was ready for the rag box. Things sometimes weren't that clear to him. One day when he dozed off, a loud bang brought him to his feet. "What the hell!" he yelled.

"The wind blew the door shut," his mother said. "You're right on the edge. You'd better take a break."

At the end of the month, Stan's check was again smaller than he expected. He called Heidi and demanded to know why.

She said, "Don't get excited. Let's go over your phone log and check the figures."

They found discrepancies, but not many.

She said, "Lately, your calls have been shorter. You need to keep reaching for those longer calls."

"I'm doing the best I can," he said. "I tell people what I see in the cards. But I don't like being shorted on my time. I'll keep reading, but I'm unhappy with the situation."

"Stan, you're doing a good job for us, but you've got to see our side of it. We have to keep up with a lot of readers, and we're bound to make some mistakes. That's only natural. We straighten things out as much as we can, but we have policies about who gets priority calls, and I can't change that. So, when you are on a call, keep your average in mind."

Stan told his mother about the conversation. When he came to the part about how minutes were averaged, he defended himself. Sure, his calls were short, but he was proud of what he was doing. "I think I've helped a lot of people. Those people at the psychic hotline are just in it for the money. The coach is criticizing my minutes. She wants my average to go up—soon—she said."

When his mother sensed the tension between Stan's desire to help people and his coach's business-like manner, she began to get a familiar feeling. Like a damsel tied to a railroad track, she thought she could see the headlights of an oncoming train.

"This is happening all over again. You never know when to keep your mouth shut. Just do your job. If the company wants you to keep customers on the line longer, it can't hurt."

"I'm not strictly their employee. They call me an independent contractor. And I really care if I help people."

―――――――――――○◅◒◦◦―――――――――――

S tan kept on putting in long days. A few people called back, some more than once, like a woman in Mississippi.

"Hello," she slurred, "Who is this?" She had called before. He knew she had called to talk. Apparently, she had money—enough to make her feel she was the target of fortune hunters. "Every man I meet just wants my money. They never love me for myself. You'd never do anything like that, would you?" she asked. "I can tell you're someone I can trust."

Stan said, "Maybe you're just looking for love in all the wrong places."

"Men are all alike," she said. "I know I've got a drinking problem, but everybody has faults. I've been to every bar in town. Why can't I meet a man more like you?" She was mumbling. "I know two people like us could be happy together." She was about to repeat her invitation for him to come to Mississippi to meet her.

"My finances right now wouldn't cover a trip like that, so that's not an option," he said.

"I'll send you the tickets. Come for a week so we can get acquainted. No commitment or anything."

When he told Dave about it, Dave said, "Hell, man, go! What've you got to lose? As long as you've got a return ticket, what's the problem?"

But Stan hesitated. A leap of faith is the act of a blind man, and Stan's eyes were not totally shut. He had a bumper sticker that read:

BALL and CHAIN

On the last day of his second month, Stan got a call from Heidi. "Stan, you're getting a lot of calls, but too many of them are short. We have a lot of expenses to cover, so we need your calls to be longer. Is there any way I can help you? Do you have any problems we could advise you on?"

"I don't know of any problems I'm having. I just do what I've always done. I lay out the cards and read 'em like I see 'em."

"That could be a problem," Heidi said. "Most people don't like to get bad news. Have any of your readings been like that?"

"Look. I can't control what cards come up. Sometimes the news is bad. But, hey, that's life. If something bad's going to happen, you're better off knowing about it, aren't you?"

"I understand where you're coming from, but if people get a message that shakes them up too much, they get leery and never call back. You're sort of slitting your own throat when that happens."

"I'm sorry. I can't lie about what I see. I always ask them if they want me to be upfront with them." If Heidi had a problem with honesty, that was her problem.

His next check should be just enough to get him into an apartment if Dave came in with him. He was sure he could put in at least enough time on the psychic line to cover his expenses. Dave would help move his stuff with his pickup, and Stan already had a girl in mind to invite over.

His check arrived the next day, and he got a call from Heidi. "Stan, you're costing the company money. We hope you can do something about your average. You should know that your job is in jeopardy. The ball's in your court now."

Stan resented hearing the same words over and over as if he were a slow kid in school. What did they expect? He could not control what the cards said. He was helping people get their lives back together.

Stan felt frustrated. He knew what the hotline people wanted him to say, but he couldn't get past his faith in the messages he saw in the cards, saying, "I only read the cards. I don't choose them."

<hr>

Although he was feeling boxed in, he spent the day packing for his move while his mother was making her rounds. In a couple of cartons, he had placed things he valued but did not use often—like his high school yearbook. His photo was on the page before the one with Dave's. Stan had dropped out near the end of his senior year, too late for them to take his picture out. The photos reminded him of his old gang although Dave was the only one he had seen in years.

Through his bedroom window, Stan saw his mother's SUV drive up. She popped the back end and began pulling her samples out. Stan knew the cases were heavier after she had wrestled them all day long. He heard her set them on the hall table with a plunk.

Stan shut the door and called the Psychic Power Network. He needed more hours, a lot more. The supervisor didn't take his call for several minutes. When he finally got through, Stan said, "I'm busting my butt out here trying to help people, and I've been putting in all kinds of hours."

"We appreciate your calling, Stan. We were just about to call you. We're going to have to let you go. Your averages have been too low for too long. We can't afford to keep you on any longer. We really wish you good luck though. Your final check will be in the mail in about two weeks. Give us a call sometime." The line went dead.

"Money-grubbers! They're all alike." He was sorry, but it seemed to be out of his hands now.

A knock on his door startled Stan. His mother poked her head in and said with a tired smile, "I guess you can't wait to move out. I think it will be nice for both of us. Don't worry about the money you've borrowed. You'll need to get on your feet first."

She closed the door, and in a few seconds, he heard the sound of the ice maker in the kitchen spitting out cubes.

He sat on his bed and stared at the floor for several minutes without blinking. With his left foot, he slowly pushed the two boxes filled with his mementos into the back corner of his closet. He hoped there was space for other things that had suddenly become only memories: his job, his hope for an apartment, his dream of barbequing, the ladies, and the open cage door, now closed.

He noticed that his left sneaker had begun to separate from the sole at the toe. He guessed he would need a new pair soon. At the front door, his hand on the doorknob, he yelled to his mother, "I'm gonna hang out with Dave for a while." To himself he said, "I'll go job hunting . . . tomorrow . . . for sure."

From Darkness to Light

I t was nighttime, and I needed to go to our outdoor toilet. I was six and scared of the dark. An older brother who used to take me was away in college. So, that left only my parents. My father, exhausted from a hard day of carpenter work, sunk into the living room rocking chair and slowly turned the pages of the evening newspaper. I was afraid to ask him, but I could ask Mother.

"Mama, I have to go to the toilet," I whispered.

"Hubby, take Wayland to the toilet," she said. "It's dark, and he's scared." *She's on my side*, I thought.

"There's nothing to be afraid of," he said firmly. "He can go by himself." His words struck fear into my heart.

He dropped his newspaper to the floor, stood up, and reached me in two steps. Grabbing my arm, he dragged me to the back door and thrust me out into the outer darkness. The door slammed, and I was alone.

There was nowhere to turn, no place to find shelter. I pressed against the house. My tears gushed out. I hated my father for being so cruel, and my mother for allowing him to take control.

After a few minutes, I ran out of tears. My eyes began adjusting to the night. Dim outlines began to appear. I had heard about ghosts and seen a few in movies.

Gradually, I made out the chinaberry tree I played under every day, its purple blossoms as sweet at night as in the day. Then, beyond it, the hen house materialized out of the darkness, its yard now empty. Soon, beyond the trees and the hen house, the bright moon's clear outlines of the outhouse at the rear of our property emerged.

There were no ghosts. I was no longer afraid.

Odd Animal Behavior

*This story is true in every detail
except for where I have slightly embellished it.*

⚬⚬⚬

Our tiny white house was situated on a dirt road at the edge of a small village in southern Oklahoma. The time was late summer, and I was probably about five years old. That meant going barefoot, playing *Hide-and-Seek* after sundown with neighborhood children, and sitting on quilts on the lawn while counting "shooting stars" across the eastern horizon.

The neighborhood men, home from work, washed and fed, were on our front porch and lawn with my dad, listening to the broadcast of Joe Louis, world champion heavyweight boxer. Glued to the set, my dad envisioned every throw and jab of left and right, while the women visited among themselves, and we children played tag and other running games.

A small, yellow-haired dog ran up, darting in and out of our small group. Perhaps I became more aggressive than I should have, or I touched it and scared it. For whatever reason, the little fellow nipped my ankle.

He didn't break the skin, but the sensation of his teeth on my flesh scared me. Infuriated, I dived for him, but he saw me coming and darted out of our yard and down the road. Finally, after about a half-block, panting breathlessly, I caught the rascal.

Holding him with both hands, I knelt and bit him back. The instant I felt his hair on my tongue, the thought popped into my mind: *My friends and all the adults in the neighborhood watched me chase the dog, grip him with both hands, and kneel to bite him.*

They must have thought, *What odd animal behavior.* And *that dog was odd, too.*

Moray

Although he did not need notes, young, distinguished professor of philosophy, Dr. Matthew Moray left for his Philosophy 101 lecture with his notebook in hand. Passing by his office wallboard, he sneered at the group photograph held there by thumbtacks. Department heads, dressed in academic robes and wearing colored hoods denoting their degrees and honors, were not in his league. Moray's was the only doctorate on the entire staff from an Ivy League school. Comparing their credentials with his was like comparing a stick figure to the Mona Lisa.

When the university offered Moray a position, he had told his wife, "I'm only taking this job because the good universities have no openings." Describing the committee who interviewed him, he said, "They need my degree to help them qualify for accreditation." Fingering his Phi Beta Kappa ring, he thought, *The head of the department will age out soon. They'll ask me to head the department. Of course, I'll accept. It's the fastest way out of a second-rate, no-name university.*

Just like me, many students are here because they couldn't get into a better school. I suppose we have that in common, he mused. His expectations were not high. Pseudo-intellectual students, eager for their first encounter with classical philosophy, flocked to his classes.

Moray swept into the lecture hall like a prince coming to claim his throne. Students filled the 285 seats, and more lined the walls, hoping others would drop the course and they could get in.

Preparing to assess his new flock of sheep, Moray arranged his notebook on the podium and looked out but not far. His gaze stopped at the front row where he caught himself gaping at a pair of shapely, crossed legs.

Raising his eyes slightly, he beheld perky breasts, a symmetrical face, and shiny hair. Crowning it all was a smile of adoration. He had seen that look before. *Probably infatuated with a person of authority*, he reasoned. *Young, impressionable girls often fall for professors.*

She came by the dais after class to ask about a point in his lecture. Her name was Cassandra. After his second lecture, Cassandra waited to ask yet another question. Moray was pleased that at least one student in the crowd showed some understanding.

One day Cassandra looked unhappy. She remained in her seat after class. He walked over to her. "Cassandra, you don't seem yourself today."

"Thanks for noticing, Dr. Moray. Things have come together to make the perfect storm," she sighed. "My bus pass expired yesterday, my bike broke down, and I had to walk to school. Now I'm dreading the walk home."

"What direction do you go?" he asked.

"I live near Parkside and Lincoln," she replied.

"That's on my way home. I could give you a lift."

"Could you? I would be so grateful."

As he drove, they chatted about his lecture on the arguments for the existence of a divine being, one of Moray's most popular lectures in the Bible belt.

She said, "I see now that the arguments don't provide any proof. They're not facts—only arguments."

He said, "I think you got the point."

When he stopped at the curb, she got out quickly and thanked him. He watched her bound up the stairs and found himself thinking, *She's cute but too young for me.*

———————⊂∞⊃———————

T wo more times Cassandra had a problem with transportation. Each time Moray dropped her off at her apartment. Class after class, she flashed her smile from the front row. *What a bright light she is,* he thought. *Most students' brains are like streetlamps that turn off automatically when the sun comes up.*

One Friday she hardly looked up the entire lecture. After the room emptied, he went to her, still seated.

"Cassandra, what's the problem?"

"It's my boyfriend," she said. "We've been together for almost two years. He told me last night he's seeing someone else. It was unexpected."

"I'm sorry to hear that," he said.

"It's not your problem," she conceded. "He gave me the usual line: He wasn't happy, he wasn't being fulfilled, and he wanted to explore other options."

"If he feels that way, perhaps you should explore other options, too," Moray said. "As pretty and smart as you are, there must be a long line of young men who would like to meet you."

"Most of the guys I know backed off after Gary and I got together. I'm not sure any of them would be interested now. Besides, I feel like I'm not the same person I was before I started taking your class." Her face lit up with admiration. "What a difference you've made in the way I think and how I understand life."

She paused and looked up at him, only a little embarrassed. "I'm stranded—again. I would accept a ride if you wouldn't mind. I could walk, of course, if you're not leaving soon."

"No problem. I'll give you a lift."

When they arrived at her apartment, she pleaded. "Would you mind coming up for a few minutes? The apartment seems so empty. Gary took all his things when he moved out."

What can be the harm? he thought. *I'll be spending a few minutes comforting a student I respect who needs someone to talk to.*

As they entered the studio apartment, she asked, "Would you like coffee, or perhaps something else to drink?"

"Coffee's fine," he said, reminding himself he didn't handle alcohol well. Brewing would take a while. As he speculated about how to fill those minutes, she sat down near him at the small table.

"Do you use cream?" she asked. "Sugar's on the table."

"I take it black." Attempting to lighten the mood, he added, "No use spoiling the taste."

She looked at him and said, "Your course has been a tremendous help. Before I met you, I was thinking about dropping out of school."

"What a waste," he said. "You have a lot to offer."

She moved closer to him, and his pulse quickened. She looked directly at him. "You're so kind and understanding. Not everyone would be so caring." She poured the coffee, and when she sat back down, inched her chair closer to his.

Moray blushed.

What's happening? Is she coming on to me? I'm almost twice her age! His face flushed, and she backed away.

"Thanks for coming up. I appreciate every minute you give me."

He rose, sighed deeply, and went out the door and down the stairs. Driving home, he thought, *That was close! I've known teachers who got caught messing around with a student. Back east, it wouldn't be an issue. But here in redneck country, it's a foolish and unnecessary risk.*

I n the foyer of his home, he met a frowning wife, arms on her hips. "Did you get the things on the shopping list?" Seeing his empty arms, she said, "You forgot again."

He thought, *Whatever happened to "Welcome home, dear, how was your day?"*

"Damn!" he said. "I'll run to the store."

"Never mind." Her tone was flat. "We'll make do with leftovers." She ferried food from the refrigerator to the microwave, and after a few minutes, called Moray to dinner.

He toyed with his food. When he looked up, she was staring at him. He had difficulty meeting her gaze. *Why am I nervous? I did nothing wrong. She's the one who's letting herself go, putting on extra weight, and nagging me. My God, has she no self-respect?*

Lying beside his wife in bed that night, Moray knew he should want her. He let his hand fall on her breast, and she turned to him willingly. But in his imagination, he was making love to Cassandra. "Cassandra" smiled. "Cassandra" admired his lovemaking. He left "Cassandra" longing for more, but his wife turned her back to him and went to sleep.

T he next day in class, looking at Cassandra, he wondered, *Did she fantasize about me last night as I did about her?*

After class, she came up to him. He knew she had yet another emergency, and she'd accept a ride home.

On the drive to her apartment, Moray felt her presence in the seat opposite him. He sensed the fullness of her figure and felt a hunger rising. For her part, she sat quietly. When they arrived, she invited him up.

Entering her studio apartment, he noticed her carefully made bed with a vase of fresh-cut flowers on the bedside table. She made no effort to open the drapes. Instead of overhead lights, she switched on a small bedside lamp. Cassandra brought a bottle of wine and two glasses to the table and poured each of them a drink.

Moray began to breathe rapidly.

Raising her glass, Cassandra said, "No other teacher has treated me like you do. I care for you. I'm aware of our age difference, but it doesn't matter. I hope you feel the same."

"I do care for you, but I wouldn't want to take advantage of you." The wine was causing him to lose his focus. "You're my student," he reminded her.

"I think I'm beyond being a student. I feel so close to you." Her face was that of an innocent kitten begging for love. "I hope it doesn't embarrass you that I find you attractive. I've never had a better teacher—or friend." She placed both her hands over his, then took one of his hands, and raised it to her cheek.

Moray felt aroused as he had not been for a long time. His adrenaline rush screamed, "*Damn the consequences! Be a man!*"

An hour later, on her bed, he said, "You're so beautiful. You've made me feel . . . well, I haven't felt this way in a long time. I feel invigorated, almost young again."

"You're wonderful," she said. "I've never felt so safe."

Cassandra's emergencies were not great, but they were steady, needing a ride home, once, sometimes twice a week. Each time, Moray was in her apartment for more than an hour. But the longer their arrangement continued, the more clearly he saw the threat it could be to his future.

The sex is great, and Cassandra is beautiful, but she doesn't fit into my plans. He rehearsed his exit like lines in a play. In Cassandra's apartment, seated at her little table, he began, "I'm feeling ashamed."

"Ashamed? Of me?"

"You? Of course, not. Of myself. I lost interest in my wife. Still—she doesn't deserve to be hurt," he said.

"What are you saying?" she asked.

"I'm saying you're gorgeous and smart, but I'm not proud of myself. I hope you'll forgive me."

Moray stood and took from his pocket a velvet-covered box, opening it to reveal a gold chain and a pendant that bore the image of his philosophy fraternity.

"I want to give you something to remember me by."

Cassandra stood with her back to him. He could not see her tears as he connected the gold chain behind her neck or her hand rising to caress the pendant.

T he following day, Cassandra came to class late, and sat in the back row, unsmiling. Perhaps she had seen their relationship growing into something more than he had. He needed to heal the wound if he could. When the students were leaving, he met her in the aisle and blocked her exit. "Cassandra, could I see you for a moment?"

"Of course, Dr. Moray," she said. The room was soon empty except for the two of them.

"Did you enjoy the lecture today?"

"Is that what you wanted to see me about?"

"Not really," he said. "I feel I've hurt you. It's entirely my fault. I want to apologize again. I hope to make it up to you. I don't know how, but I'll try to find a way."

"I don't think that will be necessary," she said. "Gary came back last night. We're back together again. He was upset when I told him about us. He said something about working it out with you. If he calls you, I think an apology will set things right."

M oray's wife was in the kitchen loading the dishwasher when the phone rang. In his study, Moray lifted the receiver and heard an unfamiliar voice. "Dr. Moray?"

"Yes."

"It's come to my attention you've been messing around with one of your female students."

"Cassandra told me you might call," Moray answered. "I apologize for any misunderstanding. I hope it's all behind us."

"You hope so," came a cold voice, "but I don't think it's going to be so easy. You can't take an apology to the bank."

"Meaning what?" Moray asked.

"Meaning one word from me, and the university could fire your ass. I'm guessing your wife wouldn't be too thrilled about it either."

"I agree my wife wouldn't be thrilled, but I doubt if it would affect my teaching career. Cassandra isn't a high school student."

"If you want to take a chance, be my guest. Otherwise, I want to hear a cha-ching soon."

"Are you trying to blackmail me?" he said.

"You catch on fast for a college professor."

"What are you suggesting?" asked Moray.

"This is not a suggestion. For starters, you'll hand over a plain envelope containing one thousand dollars in bills no larger than a twenty. When you give it to Cassie, tell her it's your gift to Gary. Do as I say, and you can keep your little job," he said and hung up.

S uddenly the specter loomed large. If he reported the attempted blackmail, his affair with Cassandra would surely be in the newspapers. He could see jobs at better universities vanishing in thin air. On the other hand, if he paid Gary, he might think he had a good thing going, get greedy, and ask for more. Moray felt like a rock climber suspended by a thin rope Gary could snip at any time, now, or in the future.

So, one week later, before the close of his lecture, Moray said, "Miss Phillips, may I see you after class?"

When all the other students had left, he took from his briefcase a plain envelope and placed it in Cassandra's hands. She had a puzzled look when he said, "Give this to Gary," but she placed the envelope in her book bag and left without a word.

He thought, *She doesn't know. But she's a smart cookie. By the time she hands this to Gary, she'll have it figured out.*

A month later, to the day, he got a call from Gary. "Time for your monthly dues," he announced.

Monthly? How long does he intend to keep this up?

Moray weighed his options and saw no immediate way out of his situation, so he began paying the sum regularly.

M onths later, in a lawyer's office, Moray asked, "Are our conversations protected by attorney-client privilege?"

The lawyer answered, "So long as the problem you mention is not a crime, and is, as you say, an indiscretion, our conversation is protected. What indiscretion have you committed?"

"It's not about me. I'm asking for a colleague. He slept with one of his students. My friend realized it was a mistake and has broken it off. Now, someone is trying to blackmail him."

"Blackmail's a crime. All your friend has to do is blow the whistle on the blackmailer," said the lawyer. "However, I'm sure you're aware in our community, any scandal would put his career at risk."

He knew he was not thinking clearly. "What if my friend got a signed statement from the woman involved saying they never had relations? Would that stop the blackmailer?"

"Just the opposite. If your friend went to the trouble of getting a legal document denying it, an investigator would ask him why he felt the need for such a document if he's not guilty. So long as the blackmailer has the affair to hold over your friend's head, the blackmailer holds the winning hand."

Moray left the lawyer's office, casting about for options. He rejected hiring a private detective to follow Gary to record his acceptance of a blackmail payment, or to see if any of his acquaintances might rat him out. Involving a detective added a new and unwelcome dimension to his puzzle.

If I had only gotten the position I deserve in a real university, this would never have been an issue. But in this conservative community, it could destroy my career or set it back light-years. Without my academic career, I have nothing. What I've dreamed of all these years is slipping through my fingers because of a sniveling two-bit blackmailer and his spineless girlfriend. He'll bleed me dry, and still not keep quiet—but not if I can secure a new teaching post before it becomes public.

S oon after he visited the lawyer, Moray heard from Gary. "Sorry to say this, Moray, but my expenses are going up, so I'll need more money next month."

Moray was growing desperate, "You're draining me dry as it is. I'm running out of resources. Have a little pity."

"Oh, yeah, I'm a pity expert, old man! You'll see how serious I am when you get back to the university."

Later, Moray passed a younger colleague in the hallway who showed Moray a small, yellow scrap of paper and said with a smirk on his face, "Moray, old buddy, what does this mean? The note says, 'Ask Moray about Cassie.'"

"Just a little inside joke. Think nothing of it," Moray responded and walked on to indicate its insignificance.

Moray walked into his office, slumped in his swivel chair, and sat staring at the floor. He had no idea where Gary might strike again, but he was sure it was coming. With no relief in sight, his anger churned like lava in a volcano. He was barely able to see to drive home.

On his doorstep was a rose with a note attached: "To M with love, C & G." Relieved he had gotten home before his wife, he threw the rose aside, crumpled the note, and stuffed it in his pocket. His mind raced. *Is there no way to stop this leech? One way or another, he'll destroy me.*

Moray threw his jacket on the sofa, trudged into his library, and withdrew the note from his pocket. Eyeing it, he poured himself a tall glass of scotch.

As the alcohol seeped into all parts of his body, ideas, like building blocks, began to come together. *If I resisted, he would laugh as he brought me down.* Moray was horrified, but as he took the last gulp of scotch, the idea overwhelmed him: *If Gary were dead, my problem would be solved.*

The word *murder* was foreign to Moray's morality, but there it was. His mind began to explore the extreme end of a list of possible solutions.

If I were to do this terrible thing, I would act the victim—which I truly am—and it would have to look like self-defense. An old man in the next block had been beaten in a home invasion recently. Burglaries in Moray's neighborhood, although sporadic, were frequent enough to justify the use of a weapon in self-defense. Of course, he could never bring himself to it, yet he couldn't control the urge that compelled him forward.

S lightly hungover the following morning, Moray removed his handgun from his bedroom closet, checked its condition, and placed it in the desk drawer in his study.

On the last day of the month, Cassandra, wearing yet another new and attractive outfit, approached him. "Cassandra, tell Gary I can't pay him this month."

She lowered her gaze and walked away quietly.

He waited by the phone. It didn't ring on the first night—or the second. On the third night, he heard the familiar voice.

"You're late with your payment. I guess I'll have to drop by the dean's office tomorrow and let him in on your little secret—maybe invite a newspaper photographer to get a nice shot of you lecturing."

"Gary," he tried to sound desperate, "you don't understand. I've withdrawn all the ready cash I have. My bank account is flat. I can get cash from my retirement funds, but not till next month. Can't you cut me a little slack?"

"I've got obligations, and I can't wait. You must have something in your house worth a grand—a painting, some jewelry, something."

"I have a gold watch."

"OK, professor. One gold watch. Don't try anything funny."

"I'm trying my best. Can you come after 11:00? My wife will be in bed. I'll leave the garden door to my office unlocked. Come alone. I want this to be just between you and me."

B y 10:30, Moray had said goodnight to his wife. He made sure the French doors to the garden were unlocked and waited in his study with the safety on his gun turned off. The knife he would place in Gary's hand would be wiped clean, bearing no evidence Moray had ever touched it.

On the tiled garden path rested a large stone that Moray planned to throw through the windowpane into the library, showing how Gary had gained entrance.

Shooting Gary in the chest would indicate Gary was coming toward him and not running away. Gary would be dead before Moray's wife woke from the sound of the gunshot and got downstairs.

As soon as the police finished their investigation and left, he would rush to Cassandra's apartment to convince her he had shot Gary in self-defense. He'd stress that if Cassandra went to the police, she would implicate herself in a felony and probably go to jail. Her only chance was to stay clear and say nothing.

Moray rehearsed questions the detective would ask:

How did the intruder get in?

"Through the door leading in from the garden."

How did he get the door open?

"He must have thrown the rock through one of the panes and stuck his hand through to unlock the door."

What were you doing when he forced his way in?

"I was in deep meditation which I do every night in the darkness before retiring. The breaking glass jarred me out of my trance. As soon as I got my bearings, I turned on the light. There was this crazy man.

Did you recognize him? "No."

What happened next?

"I was scared out of my wits. He was a lot bigger than I am. His eyes looked like he might be on drugs. He seemed startled to see someone in the room. He came at me with a knife. I jerked open the drawer, grabbed my revolver, and fired. I meant to stop him, not kill him."

What was a loaded revolver doing in your desk?

"I moved it there only two weeks ago. Since there have been problems in the neighborhood lately, I just thought of it as insurance, but I never expected to use it."

———————————————— ∞∞∞ ————————————————

And it happened like a well-rehearsed play. Gary appeared at the garden door. Moray motioned him in. As Gary approached, Moray opened his desk drawer as if to retrieve his watch, called up all his courage, and without a word, he fired. Gary fell forward in front of the desk. Moray hurried to place the knife in his hands and made sure Gary's fingerprints were on it.

Following the shot, he laid the gun on the desktop. From the garden, he threw the rock through the window and let it lie where it landed on the carpet. Then he dialed 911, identified himself, and said, "Please send an ambulance and the police. A man broke into my home and attacked me. I shot him. Please hurry!"

He placed the phone back in its cradle and waited. Hearing a noise, he glanced up at the garden door, then leaped from his chair. There stood Cassandra.

"Gary!" she cried as she bent to touch his body on the floor.

"What in hell are you doing here?" Moray barked.

"I was waiting in the car for Gary," she said. Seeing Gary's body on the floor, her face contorted. She turned to Moray and spoke barely above a whisper, "Did you shoot him?"

"I tried to reason with him, but he got angry and came at me. He might've killed me," Moray said, indicating the knife he had placed in Gary's hand.

She protested, "Gary didn't carry a knife."

The office door opened, and Moray's wife entered the room. "What was that horrible noise?" She saw the body on the floor and Cassandra, weeping. "What's going on? Who's that man—and this woman?"

Hearing the faint sounds of sirens, Moray began to panic. Ignoring his wife, he spoke firmly to Cassandra, "Get out! When the police arrive, you'll be implicated in blackmail. Leave now if you want to protect yourself."

Cassandra whined, "I don't understand."

"You don't have to understand!" he barked. "If you want to stay out of jail, leave! Now! Say nothing of this to anyone!"

On the verge of tears again, Cassandra's looked from the body on the floor, to Moray and Mrs. Moray. Moray grabbed Cassandra's arm, rushed her to the garden door, and snarled as he pushed her. "Go now, or you'll be in this deeper than you can imagine!" She limped away as if in a trance and disappeared into the darkness.

M oray turned to his wife, pleading. "The police will be here shortly. Please, just go along with whatever I tell them. Answer their questions but under no circumstance volunteer a word about the woman you saw. She is one of my students. After this mess is over, I'll explain everything."

The sounds of the approaching sirens intensified the pressure Moray felt. "Can you do that for me?"

"What's this all about?" she demanded.

"The man on the floor is a burglar!" he shouted. "When he saw me, he went crazy and attacked me, so I shot him. Tell the police about the shot you heard and what you see here.

Just say nothing about the woman, and don't mention the word 'blackmail!'"

The sirens died, and within seconds the doorbell sounded. Moray signaled to his wife to let them in. In a daze, she obeyed.

Paramedics entered, followed closely by the police. "We got a call about a shooting," said one of the uniformed officers.

"Yes, a burglar attacked me," said Moray, leading them into the library.

The paramedics' examination of the body on the carpet revealed no signs of life, so the coroner was alerted. Due to the violent nature of the death, the officers cleared the library to preserve the scene. The coroner's team arrived in hazmat garb and her photographers took a series of shots from different angles.

Finally, a short man wearing an off-the-rack suit entered. "I'm Detective Willard. Where's the body?"

Moray was still waiting in the next room as the detective examined the body and withdrew a wallet from Gary's pocket, identifying him. Willard directed an officer to do a background check. The officer entered the code on his laptop and, in seconds, reported, "Sir, the only record for Gary Dorman shows an arrest on suspicion of mugging. Never charged for lack of evidence. Nothing else comes up."

As paramedics wheeled the body out of the room, two officers entered with Cassandra in tow, holding a wadded handkerchief in her hands.

The officers said to Willard, "Sir, this woman was sitting in front of the house in a car. We asked her what she was doing here, and she couldn't explain, so we brought her in."

Moray interrupted. "Officer, this young lady is a student of mine at the university. She dropped by for tutoring."

"Tutoring at this hour?" asked Willard.

Moray glanced sideways at the detective and raised his eyebrow. "It was a special kind of tutoring."

"Oh," said the detective.

Willard turned to Moray. "Sir, tell us what happened."

Moray repeated the script he had prepared. "I was sitting in the dark, meditating. I woke up when a rock shattered the glass in the French door leading to the patio. When I turned on the light, there stood this stranger coming at me with a knife. I remembered the gun in my desk drawer and I grabbed it and shot—in self-defense. I never meant to hurt the man. He had a crazy look in his eye. I thought he might be on drugs."

"So, you don't know the man?"

"I never saw him before in my life."

Moray began to perspire. "I think I need a drink of water. Honey, would you bring me a glass, please?" Willard nodded his permission for her to leave.

She didn't move. Instead, she looked at the detective and said, "I think I prefer to stay and hear what my husband has to say."

The detective shrugged. "Let's see what the young lady has to say," he said.

"M a'am, what is your name?"

"My name is Cassandra Phillips."

"Tell us in your own words what you're doing here," Willard asked.

Her creased brow and trembling chin produced a cold sweat in Moray. His mind raced. *Will she do as I told her? Has she realized her risk of going to jail?*

Cassandra collapsed into the high wingback chair near the desk, still weeping. She lifted her face to Moray and sobbed, "I'm so sorry, professor! I've got to tell the truth!"

Moray prepared for the worst.

"I fell in love with my teacher. I've been chasing him the entire year, and he's ignored me. I came tonight to try once more, to see if he had any feelings for me at all. But it was no use; he sent me away."

Moray stifled a gasp. His wife gave him a "drop dead" look.

Willard said to Moray, "We'll wait for forensics to finish their report to determine how to go forward. Professor, Mrs. Moray, and Miss Phillips, we'll need formal statements from you at the station tomorrow. I think we have what we need for the time being."

The detectives followed Cassandra out of the house. Moray and his wife heard the cars pulling away. It was finally Mrs. Moray's turn.

She looked at her husband and said, "Now, what is this about blackmail?"

"Sit down, Honey. I have a confession," he said as he ran his thumb over his Phi Beta Kappa ring. "I had an affair with Cassandra. It was early last semester. It was brief, and it's been over for months. But, after I broke it off, her boyfriend began blackmailing me, threatening to go public. If it got out, I knew it would end my career and our chance for better things, so I paid several thousand dollars to keep him quiet.

Cassandra came tonight to collect a payment, but I told her I'd had enough. I wasn't going to pay anymore. She left. A few minutes later, her boyfriend broke into the library. He came at me with a knife, and I shot him in self-defense."

She took a few minutes to process all the information he had just given her. Her mind fell on his infidelity. "I'm not surprised you had an affair," she admitted. "I've suspected for a long time."

Her chin rose and she looked down her nose. "Why did that woman lie to the police?"

"If she admitted they came here to get money, she would face charges of blackmail. She lied to cover her butt."

"This is an ugly mess I can't make sense of. I can't believe what's happening," she shook her head. "I'm going back to bed. You get the sofa."

She'll keep quiet. But, will Cassandra? Moray wondered.

M oray finally dozed off on the sofa and went into a deep sleep. The next morning, still dressed in clothes from the previous night, he staggered into the kitchen in search of some breakfast. He drew water and started the coffee. Before the brewing had finished, he heard a car in the driveway, and his wife came in the back door.

"You're out early."

She said, "I've been to church."

"To church?" He was incredulous. "For what?"

"I went to confession," she replied.

"Confession?" The word alarmed him. "You didn't say anything about last night, did you?"

"No. Things have been bad between us for a long time. I felt neglected and pushed aside. I can't tell you how bad I felt. It turned me into a harpy."

"So, what did you confess?" he probed.

"I confessed the failure of our marriage—my failure as a wife. I should have been more supportive. You've worked so hard to get ahead. I've let you down. I'm genuinely sorry. I had a long talk with the priest. If you're willing, I want us to start all over again."

Relief swept over him like a fresh ocean breeze. "You have nothing to apologize for. I'm the unfaithful one." He opened his arms and held her as she sobbed softly.

Several days after the event, the local newspaper printed a follow-up story on the shooting at the Moray home. He was a hero. He had defended his home, the report said, just as most others would do—or would hope to do.

In succeeding months, the story disappeared from the news cycle. Moray's lectures were full. Cassandra dropped his class. Mrs. Moray lost 25 pounds and looked like her old self after a makeover and a new wardrobe befitting the wife of an important professor. She attended faculty functions, chatted up every guest there, and organized a few successful parties to boost his career. In bed, she made Matthew hum like a new Corvette. *Things,* he thought, *couldn't be better.* With less than two months left in the year, Moray received official notice the board chose him as the new head of the philosophy department.

Finally! he thought. *Light at the end of the tunnel. As head of the department, I'll have a much easier time attracting the attention of a better school. It's my ticket out of this God-forsaken desert.*

A t the end of graduation exercises, Moray and his wife attended a faculty reception where they schmoozed with the alumni, especially the rich ones.

Afterward, his wife went home while Moray wandered back to his office to luxuriate in his success. He sat alone, surrounded by boxes and files ready to be moved to the larger office of the department head.

However, in a locked drawer in his desk was an unopened letter he had received three days earlier. His hand trembled slightly as he inserted his key, pulled open the drawer, and withdrew the letter. The embossed envelope bore the insignia of his alma mater. It was not from a professor but from the dean. Moray was sure it could mean only one thing: an invitation to fill an opening, to be head of the department in an Ivy League school. He had paid his dues in this armpit of civilization.

He slid his letter opener under the flap of the envelope. Before examining its contents, he glanced up to see, coming down the hall, the familiar face of Detective Willard, followed by an assistant. He watched Willard stop to ask directions from the secretary before proceeding to his office. The door was open, but Willard knocked. Moray invited the men in and asked them to sit down.

"What can I do for you, gentlemen?" Moray remained calm.

"Well, professor, I'll come right to the point. The case of the burglar shot in your house was not so simple as we thought. Forensics showed Dorman was not high on drugs. With that theory out the window, we began searching for another angle. It took a considerable effort, professor, but we finally got access to your bank account. Our search turned up some unexplained withdrawals from your account. We checked Dorman's account for corresponding amounts and didn't find anything, but we started asking around. Turns out he's Miss Phillips' boyfriend, which she failed to mention, and her bank account showed deposits that matched your withdrawals."

Moray squirmed in his chair.

"At headquarters, we asked Miss Phillips if she could explain the large deposits each month into her account. At first, she maintained it was money her family sent her. I asked if her family would verify her story. We showed her the matching amounts withdrawn from your bank at about the same time she made her deposits. We made it clear, if this turns into something other than self-defense and she lies about it, we will charge her as an accessory. She told us about your affair and showed us an amulet that matches the ring you're wearing."

Moray tried to look disinterested. "Mr. Willard, I never denied an affair. Having an affair with a student does not implicate me in anything further."

Willard continued, "Cassandra said you invited Dorman to your home, and she waited in the car while he went in unarmed. When she heard the shot, she hurried in and saw Dorman lying dead."

"You're taking her word Dorman had no knife. It is equally possible he had a knife she was simply unaware of. Would a blackmailer go unarmed to a meeting with his victim? He was at my house. I wasn't in his. Your case is circumstantial, based on the word of a witness who invented a story that is in her self-interest. If you arrest me, and this goes to trial, and I'm subsequently found innocent, I can promise you a civil suit against you and your department for damages. Multiply my annual salary by 20 years and that's the amount I would be seeking. You can imagine the effect it might have on your career."

"I take your point, professor," said Willard, "however, the way it looks to me, your motive of self-defense might not stand up against the fact that you're the only one who stood to gain by having Dorman dead. I'm willing to bet arresting you is more likely to enhance my career than throttle it."

Willard ended with, "Professor, we're taking you in on suspicion of murder."

Willard's assistant produced handcuffs and indicated for Moray to extend his wrists. The chains rattled as the three of them filed past a wide-eyed secretary.

Entrepreneur

I am living the American dream. I'm an entrepreneur, one who undertook a new venture at considerable personal financial risk. The job required no formal training, but good instincts are helpful. I worked longer hours for less money—at least at first. I am not selling a product or service, nor making a statement about the lifestyles of others.

I have no government funding, and therefore, no government interference. I don't pay taxes. No one underwrites my business. I am boss and staff rolled into one. I set my hours and have only myself to please. I do not punch a time clock, nor do I wear a smock with a company logo on the back.

If I don't work, I don't eat. If I fail, it's all on me. Weather can be a challenge. Health care is spotty, but I take what I can get. I will never receive recognition from the Chamber of Commerce, although my business is ecologically friendly. I get my share of dirty looks from passersby, but most people ignore me.

I push a fully functioning shopping cart. I am into metal: aluminum.

If I were to make a list of philosophical ideas, my outlook on life, the list would include the following:

I deserve respect. I have value.

As I walk the streets, I consider the purpose of life.
Like most people, I have no answer.
Answers people spout to life's questions
sound a bit made up to me.

I don't ask for pity. You can't eat it,
and it doesn't make life any better.

I have a problem with loneliness,
but I can't afford the luxury
of feeling close to someone.
The potential for pain is too great.
I'm not unique in this respect.

Finally, there is the question of death and dying.
I mostly leave that to the poets,
but I have observed once you die, you're dead.
What happens to the body is of little consequence.

Who is Sylvia?

As evening neared, I sat alone at the grand piano in the dining hall of the First Presbyterian Church in downtown Fresno, warming up on their Steinway in preparation for entertaining 300 dinner guests. Through the hall's open double doors, a woman of about 45 or 50 entered wearing battered tennis shoes and soiled clothes. Gray hair jutted out on either side of a stocking cap she wore in unusually warm weather. She wove her way toward me, through the 30 large tables covered with white linen tablecloths with fine China settings. Passing the empty podium, she stopped at the piano.

Without preface, she asked, "Would it be all right if I eat with you?"

I thought, *She'll stand out like a sore thumb among the guests, some of the most influential citizens in the city. They were Christians, but would they feel uncomfortable with her in the same room, let alone at the same table? How would they treat her? And why is she asking me? This is not my party. I'm only a guest.* I was embarrassed, partly because I wasn't sure what I would have said if I were in charge.

Relieved to be free of the burden, I told the lady, "Ask her. She's in charge."

Sylvia had entered the dining room from the kitchen. With glistening black hair, a pageboy haircut, and clothes of the latest fashion, she glided across the floor with the poise and demeanor of a queen.

The hungry visitor turned and headed across the hall to Sylvia, who spotted her and met her halfway. In the center of the hall, the lady spoke. I could not hear the conversation, but Silvia's expression did not change.

I held my breath and waited, looking for some sign from Sylvia about how she was handling the imposition of an uninvited street person asking to join a semi-formal, high-class dinner.

When the lady stopped talking, Sylvia never hesitated. In one grand motion, she smiled, put her arms around the lady's shoulder, and escorted her to a seat.

The Gift

W hen the first chords of "Amazing Grace" hit my ear, something touched me. Unable to stop myself, I put down my soup ladle, and a few steps brought me to the side of the grand piano in the corner of the dining room. My heart opened and the sound flowed. The pianist found my key, and the chords he played embraced my voice. I was at home—in the lyrics, in the music.

As I reached the climax, from behind me a high-pitched voice interrupted, "Please, Shayla, could I have some more lemonade?" Looking up at me, a bib covering her chest, Alice sounded like an aged Oliver Twist.

I came to earth in an instant. I was working for minimum wage in a nursing home and was glad of it. In a few minutes, entrées and desserts would be up. The old and lame would eat, then return to their rooms or sit in the hall and watch passersby while I cleared tables and recorded how much each person ate. Good nutrition is critical for the elderly.

I turned to get Alice's lemonade and the pianist said, "You have a nice voice, Shayla. You should sing more."

I said, "Oh, I can't sing."

He said, "You sound pretty good to me. I've played for quite a few singers."

⚬⚬⚬

When I got home, I sank into an upholstered chair that had sprung its last spring years ago. Mama reigned from her newer chair to my left. I told my family what the pianist had said.

My younger brother said, "He must be crazy," and laughed himself into the kitchen. My sister rolled her eyes. Mama sighed and said, "Baby, different folks have different gifts. You'll find yours."

I thought, *Could waiting tables in a nursing home be my gift? I like the patients and the people I work with. I make a lot of patients smile.*

⚬⚬⚬

The following day, five minutes before the door opened for lunch, the food was ready, and bibs rested beside each plate. Residents can't come in until a CNA is present, in case someone chokes on food or has an attack of some sort. Marvin, at the piano, said, "You got time to belt one out?"

I thought, *Why not? What have I got to lose?*

He played the opening chords of "How Great Thou Art," one of Mama's favorites. The song swept me along like a bird winging its way through the air.

"I like your voice. Perhaps you could do something with it."

"Like what?" I asked.

"Like sing."

I said, "Nobody thinks I can sing."

Still fresh in my mind were the words of the music director at New Harmony Church. Eight of us were practicing a gospel arrangement, backed by a small band. In the middle of "The Road to Glory," a message of hope, my voice was moving up and down like a ship in a storm. The leader motioned me aside and said, "Shayla, I'm sorry. You're not fitting in. You can't seem to keep the beat." I was crushed.

I was singing what I felt, feelings I have only when I sing. The choir was dead silent. I was afraid to even look up as I took my coat off the hanger and dragged myself out the front door.

———————————— ∞ ————————————

T he third time Marvin invited me to sing, I didn't know what I would sing, I just knew I would do it. After the drinks and soup were out, there were a few minutes before the entrées arrived. I went over to the piano and said, "Marvin, I'd like to try again, but we have to do it quickly. I don't want to get fired for goofing off."

Marvin smiled and said, "Fine. Let's do it." As his hand swept up the keyboard, I began to sing "Stormy Weather." Whoever wrote that song knew how a storm on the inside and a storm on the outside are alike.

When the song ended, the patients broke out clapping, like I was doing a concert at Carnegie Hall. I felt proud and embarrassed at the same time.

———————————— ∞ ————————————

A t home, I told my family about singing and the patients clapping. "Sure they clapped," said my brother. "They were glad you stopped."

My sister reminded me old people don't hear well. "They like anything that makes a sound."

"Baby, you might not be as smart as your brother, or as pretty as your sister . . . " and I thought, *Here comes a backhanded compliment,* " . . . but you work hard. You know all those old people by name. You style your hair nicely. You know how to dress. You have a sweet smile, and your teeth are the whitest in the family."

"But what about my voice, Mama? Do I sing as bad as my brother and sister say? You're a good singer. What do you think?"

"It don't hurt to try, Baby, but you gotta remember we need all three checks from you kids to keep this house going." Mama's eyes were pleading. "Just don't do anything to get fired." Medicare only paid for part of Mama's medicine. Her high blood pressure was hard to control, so we couldn't scrimp on medicine.

During lunch the next day, I asked Marvin, still seated at the piano, if I could talk to him after the tables were cleared. "How would you describe my style?"

He didn't hesitate. "Your style is gospel."

"Gospel? What do you mean?" I asked.

"Traditional singers sing the notes on the page. Gospel singers add notes from their hearts. They sing all over the page. But the good ones also respect the music. They know what they're doing when they add extra notes," he explained. "Your style is definitely gospel."

"'Stormy Weather' isn't gospel."

"It doesn't have to be religious. Everything a gospel singer feels emotionally can show up. You could use a little rehearsal," he added, "and some exposure. I can help you if you want to give it a go."

We began meeting after work. He taught me how to sing "Amazing Grace," what he called "straight." He said, "Tell your heart to take five. Let your mind get a grip on the song as it was written 250 years ago. When you get the bones of the song in place, then you can improvise to your heart's content." That's putting "meat" on the bones, as Marvin put it. People can still hear the tune within the notes you sing.

He was right. It took an hour a day for two weeks, but it worked. I could go wherever my voice and heart led me and still hold onto the melody. Marvin said, "I think it's time we take this on the road. You think you're ready?"

I felt more confident. Perhaps he knew of a small church where I could sing. "If you think so, I'll try."

"I'll ask my pastor if I can bring in a soloist. I'll let you know the date."

The next day, he told me, "In two and a half weeks, it's on, if you're free."

I wasn't sure if I should invite my family. They didn't know I had been rehearsing. They might refuse to come, for fear they'd be embarrassed.

W hen the day came, I told them I was going to church, but not which church I was going to.

I had never seen the First Presbyterian Church before. Its size scared me. It was eight or ten times bigger than my church. Their parking lot was filled with row after row of cars, and Marvin walked me in the back door. In royal blue robes with white stoles, a huge choir filed past us into the sanctuary. I waited behind the stage with Marvin until it was time for me to sing. "Butterflies in the stomach" didn't come close to what I was feeling.

Marvin walked out and sat at the Steinway grand piano. He nodded, and I walked out on the stage and stood at the microphone. The room got deathly quiet. When I looked up, I saw nothing but vanilla, a couple of Orientals perhaps, nothing Hispanic. Not a black face anywhere, and not a single smile. *Had I accidentally come to a funeral?*

Marvin's long intro gave me time to get a grip, and time for the audience to get ready for some music with a beat. I sang only three notes when eyes began to turn to me like searchlights. They zeroed in on me like I was either a stack of gold or the bubonic plague—which, I couldn't guess. I sang "Amazing Grace" the way they probably never heard it. To me, it was like a rich cake with great globs of frosting. I only hoped they were eating it up.

When I came to the end, Marvin lifted his fingers from the keyboard. I couldn't read the faces. I held my breath for a short lifetime, refusing to let them stare me down. Then two hands came together, then four, then 40, then 400. I could hardly breathe. The air sparkled with excitement. I had done it.

After the closing prayer, their choir director said, "You have a wonderful gift. Thanks for coming." A lot of their members came and shook my hand. Marvin walked me to my car and gave me an envelope.

T he road home had the same chuckholes, and I hit a lot of them, but I felt like I was riding on air. Wait till my brother and sister hear. Mama will be proud of me.

"I sang a solo in church this morning," I announced before settling into my chair.

"Oh, Baby. I told your sister we should've gone with you."

My little brother said, "Count me out. I've got enough problems without that."

"Why didn't you tell us?" my sister asked. "Maybe we could've talked you out of it. How do you feel?" I laid the envelope on the table.

"What's this?" she said, opening the envelope. "This check is from a Presbyterian church."

Mama took the check. It was for as much as I earned in a full day at the nursing home.

"Yes, Marvin from the nursing home took me to his church. They pay people who sing there. When I finished, they clapped for me like it was halftime at the Super Bowl."

My little brother came over and picked up the check. He stared at it and shook his head. "There's gotta be an explanation. They must've paid you *before* you sang. It's gotta be a fluke."

Momma got a determined look on her face. "A fluke? A fluke? We'll just see. You ask your friend Marvin if he'll come to our church and play for you. We'll just see."

Mama's been a deaconess at our church forever, and when she asks, you can be sure the pastor listens.

"Let me talk to our choir director," said the pastor. Later, he called. "Sister, it took some convincing, but we're willing to trust your judgment. Should we have Shayla sing at the evening service? We have a much smaller attendance in the evening. You know what I'm saying? What do you think?"

Mama said, "Considering the size of the check Shayla brought home from that church uptown, I think, Sunday morning."

I waited in our parking lot for Marvin, just as he had waited for me at his church. I thought he would come early, but when the service began, he was still not present. I heard the hymns, the prayers, and then the animated voices of the children's choir. *Maybe I'm not as good as I thought. Maybe Marvin has chickened out.* When the gospel chorus began, the offering was being taken. My solo was next! *Where was Marvin?*

The Gospel Chorus reached the climax of their number as Marvin pulled into the parking lot. "Sorry. I've never been in this part of town before. The streets are all unfamiliar to me and I couldn't find a soul to ask for help. I wasn't too good at following your directions. But I made it!" he said as we rushed toward the door.

There's no back door to get into our church auditorium, no secret alcove behind the stage. You have to come in the front and walk down one of the aisles. Everybody can size you up as you make your way. When I walked in nobody stirred but when Marvin came following behind me, heads turned. A stranger was in our midst.

Before we could sit down, the choir director announced my solo, sounding like he was apologizing for an approaching train wreck. Marvin went straight to the piano. He gave me his prize-winning smile and nodded before beginning his introduction. As soon as the congregation recognized what he was playing, a soft humming began to fill the room. "Amazing Grace" was familiar ground.

He paused and I began. As I continued, faces around the room began to light up like Christmas lights. Hands began to move in rhythm to the music. Eyes turned skyward. Deacons chimed in with warm "Amens." And when I finished, hands clapped, and Mama glowed. My sister sat stunned. My little brother looked around not believing what he was hearing and seeing.

Walking Marvin out to our parking lot, I regretted I couldn't put a check in his hands as he had done for me. Our church pays our pastor, but not musicians.

Before I could apologize, he said, "I have a bit of news for you. When you sang for my church, we had a visitor from Los Angeles. He's in the music business. He said he'd like to hear more from you. It might be nothing, but who knows? I think you have a gift."

And I thought, *Maybe I have two gifts.*

The Rabbit and the Fox

There was a baby rabbit whose mother and father had died. He was all alone in the world. The baby rabbit did not know he was a rabbit, so he set out to discover who he was. He hadn't gone far when he heard a sound. His ears shot upward. He stood up on his hind legs, eyes fixed, still, and silent.

Down the road came a fox, smiling smugly. He looked smart to the little rabbit.

"Good morning!" said the fox. "What are you doing in the road at this hour of the day?"

"I have no mother or father. I'm alone," confided the baby rabbit, "and I don't know who I am."

"You don't know who you are?" said the fox to the rabbit. Seeing a chance to have some fun, the fox said, "You're a spider."

"A spider?" said the rabbit. "And what do spiders do?"

"Spiders spin webs, like that one over there," said the fox, pointing to a beautiful web on a nearby plant.

"Thank you," said the grateful rabbit, moving to take a closer look at the web. The fox smiled, shook his head, and ran off into the forest.

—∞∞∞—

S earching for strands to make a web, the rabbit found only long stems of grass. He worked hard trying to weave the stems into a web but failed. Disheartened, he began to nibble on the grass and scratch in the ground when along came a spider. The spider asked, "What are you doing?"

The rabbit replied, "I'm trying to spin a web. You see, I'm a spider."

"You're no spider," laughed the friendly spider. "I'm a spider. Watch. I can spin a web in no time at all." And he did.

The spider decided to amuse himself. "I saw you scratching the ground. Perhaps you're a bird. Birds scratch the ground, and they fly in the air." And the spider went back to spinning his web.

—∞∞∞—

T he rabbit liked scratching in the ground. He soon had a hole that was warm and comfortable. Then he decided to flap his ears up and down as fast as he could, to see if he could fly.

A passing sparrow saw the rabbit and lit on a nearby branch. "What are you doing?" chirped the curious sparrow.

"I'm a bird. I'm trying to fly," replied the rabbit, still wildly flapping his ears.

"You're no bird," said the sparrow. "I'm a bird. Watch. See how easily I can fly?" And he did.

Said the rabbit, "A fox told me I was a spider. A spider told me I was a bird. If I am not a spider and not a bird, can you tell me who I am?"

Said the kind sparrow, "Who you are is a question you must answer for yourself."

Moral

I f you let others tell you who you are, you will waste your life doing tasks for which you are not well suited. You must look within and find your own true nature.

And let's face it, if you're taking advice from a fox or a spider, you should be examined by a qualified psychologist.

From the Pages of the Iliad

W hile reading Homer's *Iliad*, in the original Greek, of course, I turned a page, and a curious figure popped up in the chair across from my desk.

"Hello. I'm here, not by happenstance, but when you happened on the heart of Homer's *Iliad*, I was hailed to hand you your heart's desire, and if need, to offer you my heartfelt help."

Astounded to be addressing an image that appeared out of nowhere, I said, "As a child, I read stories about genies popping out of bottles, granting wishes, and becoming slaves of the ones who rubbed the bottle—always by accident, of course. But when you magically appear and tell me you can grant me a wish simply because I've opened a dusty book, you can understand my skepticism. I could be asleep. You could be a dream or a hallucination. I haven't the slightest idea where you came from or how you got into my study."

The figure before me appeared solid. It spoke. "Indeed, I understand your justifiably judicious judgment that someone is joking with you. TV shows and lotteries entice people in a fog of flimflam going as far back as ill-fated King Midas. He was thrilled that everything he touched turned to gold until he kissed his only daughter on the cheek and—no more daughter, no more heir, no more loving family. If you need a longer bibliography, think about Jack with his magic beans."

I smiled indulgently. "Do you have a name?"

"Creatures like me do not have fixed names. We can choose any name we like and change it at will. Today I like the name Tarot," he said. "I know you're Keir McGregor. I could write a short bio on you. You worked as a lifeguard. A few years into your adulthood you chose the path of a scholar, and you now teach classics at the university."

I smiled. "So, am I in some sort of fantasy world?" He continued, "Am I supposed to ask you to do some impossible feat to show your powers?"

"You could, but that would be a wanton waste of your one wish."

"Only one, not three?"

"Three is traditional, but times are tough—the economy being what it is," spoke Tarot. "There are limits to what you can wish for. I can't time travel—go back and prevent the assassination of Lincoln or change the outcome of the Vietnamese War. I can only act in the present. I can't kill someone you hate or bring someone back from the dead, like your grandfather." His hands did a flourish and a small puff of smoke drifted upward. His eyes twinkled, but in fact, nothing else happened.

"OK. I'll go along with it. What *can* you grant?"

"I can do healings, what were once called exorcisms—bring a bitter body a better spirit. If you know someone who's a pest, I can fix that. I can also grant or take away material goods. If you want to make someone rich, including yourself—or poor—I can do that."

I shrugged and thought, I *might as well have fun with this as long as it lasts*. "You know, you don't *look* like a genie. You're not dressed in a turban and pantaloons or sporting a handlebar mustache. You didn't float up out of a bottle."

"I dress for the times. For good or ill, I'm here now because you decided to read the *Iliad*, and you came to page 132. I'm bookmarked there. I can assume you're interested in Greek poetry."

"You're right. I teach at the university. I'm a fan of all things Greek," Keir said. "Regarding the wish, how long do I have to make up my mind?"

"Any reasonable amount of time is all right. Most people select from the great trilogy: wealth, fame, and power, the most popular being wealth. But it turns out that many can't manage money smartly, and after a month or more, they're mooching money on Main. Coming into wealth revealed they had little common sense to begin with."

"I've heard of cases like that and, trust me, common sense is not one of my strong suits," said Keir.

"The pecuniary power of the purse doesn't change a person. Possessions are not always partnered with prudence, so please, if you're thinking about wealth, consider who you really are."

"I know who I'm not. I'm not a shaker or a mover. I've never stayed in a five-star hotel or flown on a private jet. Or had servants to cater to my whims."

"At least you're aware of a wider world than the one you now occupy. So, did this awareness change your views towards wealth and material things?"

"Wealth wouldn't make my top ten," said Keir.

"You have a doctorate. Perhaps you would like to enroll in MENSA and exhibit your elevated erudition among the elite."

"I don't think a high IQ would impress the few friends I have," Keir said. "Degrees mean something, but a piece of paper doesn't make anyone wiser or more useful."

The genie scratched his head. "I like your distinction between education and wisdom. Solomon asked for wisdom. He got that, plus wealth and power, and more trouble than he could handle. It didn't pay off for him." Tarot paused and squinted his eyes. "This might take a while, so I'm off to Wonderland to await my next project." And he vanished.

The dust on my badly worn book lay undisturbed. I half expected to smell burning sulfur or hear the eerie laughter of a madman, but there was nothing. I was alone.

W as I going bonkers? What if this guy is for real? I had to get out, so I took my usual 15-minute walk to The Land of Oz where Joe and I share a beer weeknights. He was waiting for me, elbows propped on the bar. We settled in a booth. "Joe, if a magic fairy came along and granted you a wish, what would you wish for?"

"I would need three wishes," he replied without hesitation. "First, I would choose the ability to heal people. I would hold a person's hand for 30 seconds. Nothing would happen, and people would laugh at me and make fun of me. But the next day, after I was long gone, the person would suddenly realize he was healed. Then they'd come looking for me to help other people, but I'd have moved on."

I said, "That's not bad. You could help a lot of sick people. But isn't the *healing hands* thing a bit weird?"

"I never mentioned it to you but, before we met, I used to go to a little charismatic church in Ashton with my friend Dave. God used me to heal people. I was young and healthy. I was laying hands on people and the healing was happening. It was cool."

"So, what happened? Did it just stop or fade away?"

"It did, and I don't know exactly when or why. My beliefs got all garbled."

"Besides being able to heal, what's your second wish?"

"I'd like to win the lottery. I'd help people with the money but keep enough to live on and travel. I'd meet some people, pay some bills, buy them a few things, and move on. I wouldn't put cash in their hands, because there's no telling how they might spend it, and I'm not into supporting anyone's habit."

I marveled. "What would your third wish be?"

"Health. I would like to have good health until the day I die, and then die naturally. I don't want to live forever, but I'd like to be healthy till the end. How about you, Bro? What would you do with your three wishes?"

"I'm thinking it over. I like your idea of helping and healing others, but it sounds a bit bizarre."

Joe said, "If you started healing and got well known for it, you could start a church, get on TV, and put on a show. You've already got the Southern drawl." Joe always said I had *the south in my mouth.*

Walking home I thought about Joe's three wishes. If I wished for wealth, I'd wish for more than I could count. But wealthy people live in a self-imposed prison to protect themselves from good-time friends, scam artists, and the crazies. They probably have more bodyguards than the President. I don't envy Bill Gates or Warren Buffet. Perhaps I was asleep the day they passed out greedy genes.

T he following day, I again opened the *Iliad* to page 132, and in an instant, there he was. "Hello, again. Have you come to a decision yet?"

"You really are real. Okay, whatever. I am reluctant to choose wealth. I have no confidence that I could handle it, and not much of a *yen* to try."

"And you a humanities professor," laughed Tarot, appreciating my pun, although I expected a groan. "You've made a wise decision, or a non-decision, as the case may be. I'm glad you don't gravitate toward greed." He paused. "How about fame, notoriety? Do you want to be an actor, painter, author, musician . . . ?"

"I've thought of acting, I've tried painting and music, but I think my strongest passion is to be a writer. There is something about the ability to mold thought that has interested me for years. I haven't mastered the skill, but I can tell when it's missing in something I'm reading."

The genie lowered himself into an overstuffed chair facing the desk and asked, "What would you write about? Do you have anything in mind?"

"It would have to have a universal theme: love, life, death, the human condition, perhaps a sweeping saga with a universal theme. How are you at editing?"

"I've edited a few titles you would recognize," said Tarot, "but none lately. What draws you to this option?"

"The idea that when I die, I would like to live on—not like a spirit in 'heaven,' or a ghost. I'd like to know that my words are on people's lips long after I'm dead—like Shakespeare or Dickens."

"You might not need my help to achieve that goal."

"Imagining ways to use my wish makes me think of possibilities I never dreamed of. I've wondered if 'none of the above' might be the best answer. I have a lady I feel strongly toward; I have a few close friends; my job is as secure as tenure can make it. I have more wealth than 95 percent of the world's population. I live in America. What's wrong with *that* picture?"

"You'd be passing up an opportunity to get out of your safe zone, a chance to see what the unknown might bring to your life. There are challenges you could meet head-on instead of waiting for life to come to you."

I smiled. "Isn't life on the edge reserved for the young? They're immortal. They can't die. They live for the moment, and I'm past that point in my life."

"You might be, but from my perspective, that would be a tragedy. To live a life with no more surprises, no more ah-ha moments, no more blazing points of light. It sounds like settling," said Tarot.

"I'll give it some thought . . ."

And the genie was gone again.

C lara and I went to the beach where we met when we were both lifeguards. Besides her great body, she is beautiful and smart.

"You take the food," I said. "I'll bring the towels and umbrella. Today's a good day. The surf's not high, so we have the beach to ourselves."

I perched on a large towel with Clara stooping behind me. As she applied sunblock to my back, she asked, "What's the mystery you were going to tell me about?"

I told her all about Tarot. She said, "That sounds crazy—a little man jumping out of a book. Sheesh."

"This is serious. If you saw Tarot, you wouldn't laugh. That you would not do."

"Then I must see the little man who pops out of a book. Even then, I might not believe it," Clara said.

"I love that about you. Practical. Skeptical. Come home with me. I'll see if I can scare up my little friend. Then we'll send him away so we can have some privacy."

"If you think you're going to have any 'privacy' with me when there is a ghost that might pop up at any time, you've got another *think* coming," she said.

"I'll race you," I said. She jumped up and ran ahead of me. The sea was only a bit chilly. My strokes were longer than Clara's, but I stayed beside her until we had swum out for a half hour.

"Time to turn back," I yelled. Another 30 minutes and we walked up on the beach. A gentle wind warmed us, and we dried off quickly. Comfortable on the towel under an umbrella, I looked at Clara, lying on her back, eyes closed, hands across her belly. *I am one lucky guy*, I thought. I wanted her, but I was content to love her with my eyes.

Clara was silent on the short drive into town. Finally, she said, "If you summon your little friend, and he doesn't appear, I'll have to have you certified." I know she meant it as a joke, but I admit it made me nervous. *What if Tarot failed to appear? What would Clara think of me then? Could Clara be right? Am I going mad?*

<hr />

I should not have worried. As soon as Clara got seated, I opened *The Iliad*, and Tarot appeared for the third time. "Good day, good professor and . . . goodness! You must be the gorgeous girl he graciously described."

Blown away, Clara's eyes darted back and forth, to him, to me, back to him, and back to me.

Tarot said, "Please, Clara, don't be afraid or puzzled. I'm sure Keir has told you all about me. Being a trained scholar, he probably got it right."

"I'm flabbergasted. I don't know what to say," said Clara.

Tarot said, "You need no words. Wait, watch, and wonder." Then he turned his attention to me. "Keir, have you decided how to use your wish?"

"Sorry to disappoint you, Tarot, but no, I haven't decided but, since Clara has seen you, she can help me explore the possibilities."

"Fine. Can I assume that you'll accept and appreciate my absence for a season? Your hesitation allows me time to take on another case, not nearly as complicated as yours. A day or two should do it." And he was gone.

"You heard him, Clara. He won't be back for a day or two." I extended my hand. She took it and followed me down the hall. And we had some privacy.

The next morning, I hit the shower and shaved. The aroma told me Clara had fixed one of her fantastic breakfasts. On these occasions, we cast all dietary cautions aside. Still in our robes, we feasted on omelets, hash browns, orange juice, French toast with maple syrup, bacon and sausage, hot coffee. The food is plain, like I like it, except for the omelets. Clara empties my refrigerator crisper drawer. If it's not nailed down, she works it into the mix. They are never the same twice, and they're always five-star.

In the middle of French toast, I said, "Thanks for breakfast. You've outdone yourself. But to turn to the topic, what are your thoughts about Tarot and the wish?"

"I can hardly believe I'm taking this 'wish' thing seriously," she said. "Genies are not real. This is a scientific world. Some people have paranormal experiences, but not me. This has me stumped. I wouldn't give it a second thought; except I saw him appear and disappear with my own eyes. Maybe we're both crazy."

She raised a bite of omelet to her lips, and I wanted to kiss them. I looked her straight in the eye. She knew what I was thinking.

"Eat your breakfast," she said. "Keep your mind on the subject."

"What if my wish is to be the world's greatest lover?"

"Why wish for what you already are?" she replied. "But sadly, I've got to go to work."

That evening at the bar, I said, "Joe, I want to bounce something off you. I'm going to tell you a story. You tell me how to end it." I told Joe everything.

As the story unfolded, his eyes got bigger and bigger. He said, "Keir, you believe one of your fantasies may actually happen? And you're not sure you want it?" I could almost see his brain running like a kid on the loose in a candy store. Finally, he spoke. "Give it to me. I'd run with it."

"Transferability never came up. I'm asking you to help me with my decision."

"If you don't want it, man, I do."

"Joe, can you focus for a few minutes?"

"Okay, I give. Not transferable. What about wishing for something like world peace?"

"Frankly, I think it might last about one day, then we'd be back to what we call normal. The same thing for wishing everyone to be healed. The next day, some kid at soccer practice falls and breaks his leg. I can think of nothing to wish for that wouldn't fall victim to our humanity. Human life can't be perfect, and perfect life is no longer human."

Joe's eyes were gleaming. The wheels were turning. The imp in him was ready to spring. "Then how about working the other side of the equation? Not the human side, but the other side?"

"You mean—what? Making a wish that affects Tarot?" I had to take a deep breath. "Man . . . that's mind-blowing!"

Joe said, "Think you could bring Tarot into the real world?"

"Tarot as a human? Without his powers? Is it possible?"

At my desk near sundown, watching the bookshelves on the opposite wall gradually grow dimmer, I strategized about how to approach Tarot. Sitting in solitude until the room was dark, I tried to anticipate Tarot's reactions. I dialed the lamp on my desk to its lowest setting, took The *Iliad* from the shelf, and placed it unopened before me. My brain was spinning with possible scenarios when I opened the book to page 132. When he appeared, I closed the book.

"Keir, my boy. You've had copious time to cogitate, so what conclusion have you come to? I've told my colleagues about your conundrum, and they found it captivating, a first for us. Our clients rarely resist a call to wealth or power."

"Tarot," I told him, "what if—just what if—I wished for you to become human?"

"Whaat?" he gasped. "Are you messing with me?"

"Do I have the power to wish you into human form?"

"I'm frightened by an unfamiliar feeling. I must fly." He said, frowning at the closed book. He pleaded, "Please, Keir, open the book."

"First, tell me if it's possible."

"I don't know for sure. I've heard the lore about a lad in the library of a noble Latvian family. One of his father's tomes accidentally toppled and fell open, ejecting one of my colleagues. The maid picked up the book, closed it, and returned it to a top shelf. My colleague had no escape. In a state of despair, the boy through tears wished my colleague were his pet and would stay with him forever. According to the story, my colleague instantly became a wolfhound that never left the boy's side. By the time the boy became a man, the wolfhound had reached old age. The pet died, and no one has heard from him since. However," he added, "I'm not sure that answers the question."

"If it helps, I think of you as an equal, not as a pet."

"You know you're talking incarnation, don't you? There are stories about spirits taking human form, the most famous in the Western world being Jesus."

"Do you believe those stories, Tarot?"

"All cultures have incarnation stories. There's no way to verify them. My colleagues and I live in the present. For us to probe the catacombs of the past is pointless."

"Imagine, Tarot. you could know the joys and pains, the highs and lows of what it means to be human. As a perk, if you still had superpowers, you'd be a hero. Stores would sell your action figures."

"And you think that's better than what I do now?"

"Perhaps. You wanted me to get out of my comfort zone. How about you getting out of yours?"

"Please, Keir, open the book. I must discuss this with my colleagues."

"Do I have your word you'll return?" I asked.

"I must. I can't leave an assignment unfinished."

At the opening of my book came a whooshing sound, and he left. I had no idea how long it might be till Tarot returned.

No matter. I decided Joe and Clara and I needed a conference—to anticipate the consequences of Tarot's becoming human. We should spend time imagining what it might mean to him.

"**D**o you want a beer, Clara?" I asked as we slid into a booth opposite Joe.

"No way, not if I intend to get any thinking done. Perhaps you guys should go light, too."

"Beer has no effect on Joe. If anything, it loosens up the hinges and gets his brain operating faster and more efficiently," I said.

"I'll take that as a compliment," said Joe, "no matter how you meant it."

Clara said, "If we assume it's possible for Tarot to cross over, shouldn't we ask how Tarot feels about it? Shouldn't he be part of our conversation? We're considering changing his whole universe, not just his body."

Joe said, "We're meddling in his life like he's meddled in others' for his entire existence."

I was concerned. I had grown to like Tarot, including his affinity for alliteration. If he crossed over, would he be lost to me forever? "If I met him somewhere, how would I know it was Tarot?" I asked.

Clara said, "When and if you meet him as a human being, your best hope of recognizing him in a stranger is if the first sentence out of his mouth contains a string of alliterations."

"Of course." I decided. "I'm going to do it—wish for Tarot to become human."

Joe said, "You've got to let us watch."

"No, I think not. We have no way of knowing what will happen. If anyone gets hurt, it should be me, not you."

I waited for Tarot in my study. The *Iliad*, open to page 132, was clearly visible. Just like before, without warning, he was there.

"Tarot, welcome back, buddy! How was your meeting with your colleagues? Did you get any answers?"

"I did not. They were as puzzled as you, Clara, and Joe were at your meeting. Yes, I was eavesdropping. At first, when I told my colleagues about your decision to forego your wish and your reasons for doing so, they laughed and hooted you were probably the most foolish person who ever lived. They said, 'You're kidding. Surely, he'll not reject this chance to have a dream come true. In all the history of time, no one has ever refused us, even those who eventually bemoaned their choice. At least they tried.'"

I laughed. "So, your colleagues agree, some of their clients should have said no, like I'm saying? Now that's funny."

"Funny to you, perhaps, but not to me. We don't have what humans call resumes, but we have records. If you refuse my offer, this will reflect badly on me. Our Leader was infuriated. You should have heard him, 'Who does he think he is? This man who's saying no to the chance to do something fantastic?' The discussion was heated but, eventually, the group voted to give you an award for being the wisest person we ever encountered. You choose—a million dollars, good health, or fame. You'd be our hero."

"Sorry to disappoint you and mess up your record, Tarot, but I've made up my mind."

Tarot's eyes darted back and forth like a trapped animal's. "Then at least give me the satisfaction of an explanation," he said shaking his head. "I just don't get it. Everybody wants something out of reach. This is like finding a stash of cash on the sidewalk. You pick it up, you're amazed at the amount, no one else is anywhere around. Do you put it down and walk away?"

"Sorry, Tarot," I said. "My mind is made up."

He continued. "Frankly, I'm mortified. If you morph me into a man, who knows what may follow?"

"This will be one hell of an experiment, my friend. Hang on to your hat." I could see the stark terror in Tarot's eyes. "Tarot, with all my goodwill and with highest hopes, I now wish for you to become human."

What followed was an eerie scream. I tried to come up with a metaphor to describe it to Clara and Joe. I compared it to the shriek of a child suddenly frightened by a monster in a nightmare, the yelp of a man in a forest attacked by a grizzly, and a soldier screaming after his legs are blown off in battle. But those sounds combined still did not capture the gut-wrenching din I heard.

After the racket, the silence was so thick, I felt like I was being crushed by it. I gasped. Was I inhaling fire? My throat burned. Then, just as quickly, it was gone, and so was Tarot. The room seemed normal, with my copy of the *Iliad* still open to page 132.

When Joe and Clara came over later, I said, "There was a *scream* when Tarot disappeared," and at the word *scream*, I shuddered.

Clara was holding my hand. "Keir, you're trembling. What's the matter?"

"I was just reliving the moment, I guess." Surely, I thought, Tarot must show up, somewhere, and soon. I waited for days that grew into a week. A second week I waited, and a third. Still nothing. After four weeks, I began to doubt I'd ever see Tarot again. Joe was peeved. "You wasted your wish. I would have done something with it. Now it's gone and we'll never know what became of it."

What could I say? I said goodbye to Clara and Joe and flew out to Los Angeles for a meeting of humanities professors, thinking, *Perhaps when I return, we'll meet Tarot, and our circle of friends will grow by one.*

O ut of the 2,000 attending the conference, I joined about 20 for a Greek seminar. Some people sleep through a lecture on the shades of differences between *agape, eros,* and *phileo,* but not me. The differences between divine love, human love, and brotherly love give insights into the Greek texts, all hidden behind the word *love* in English translations. The presentation was basic Greek, but the speaker had some good illustrations.

In the middle of the lecture, a professor type—there is such a thing—probably a few years older than me, entered and sat next to me. He put down plastic bags filled with an array of the kind of books vendors hand out at these affairs in the hope one might catch a professor's eye, and be adopted as a text or added to their required reading list. The newcomer seemed as interested in the speaker's analysis as I was.

Afterwards, others left, but he stayed. Extending his hand, he said with a slight accent I was unable to identify, "Hi. I'm Professor Theodore Tarotolli, Teddy for short. I teach at Trent University. And you are . . ."

What did I just hear? Five 'T's? Theodore, Tarotolli, Teddy, teach, Trent? "I'm Keir McGregor. Greek literature is my field. I don't think we've met."

"No wonder. The number of people delving into Greek literature diminishes daily, don't you think?"

My heart skipped a beat. Did I dare ask? "Professor, tell me about your background, where you're from, and how you became interested in Greek literature."

"I was born in Italy. I went to school first in Switzerland, and then to Cambridge, where I read the classics. After finishing my course and graduating with honors, I received a letter inviting me to interview for a position at Trent. Right off the bat, I was hired, and they made me the chair of their humanities department."

"How long have you been teaching there?"

"I just started this term."

"So, a year ago, you were at Cambridge?"

"Oddly enough, I'm not sure. Everything I've told you so far can be verified by records I found among my things, but the details surrounding the events have escaped my memory. One should know more about his past than one finds on papers in his suitcase, shouldn't one? A psychiatrist told me I had a rare form of amnesia that blocks out details of one's life but leaves one with the academic knowledge one has acquired. So, I am quite proficient in Greek even though I remember no details about my education or my past except what I find on transcripts and legal documents."

"What about your name, Tarotolli?"

"I researched it on Ancestry.com. My name is unique. If I have no children, the name will be lost to history so far as their records go."

"Let me take you to dinner, Professor Tarotolli. We must get better acquainted.

One String Banjo

B rother Jim glanced from his car window as he passed under the eight-foot neon sign with JESUS SAVES in red on the crossbar. The smell of rain was in the air. Men in dark, soiled clothes under layers of jackets waited in line on the sidewalk to enter the mission, their backs turned to the wind. He drove into the parking lot of the Dade County Rescue Mission.

Brother Jim and his group, six men and four women, left their cars and chatted among themselves as they entered the chapel through a rear door. Walking to the stage, they stayed close, like sheep in a new pasture, and fixed themselves in the light blue plastic chairs provided for guests who conducted the services.

While they waited, the men on the sidewalk inched up a narrow brick stairway, stepped through the door, and waited under a glaring fluorescent light while a staff member assigned each a bed. With a number tag in hand, they continued into the chapel to wait for the service to begin. Attendance was a prerequisite for receiving a hot meal and a bed for the night.

Two large paintings dominated the walls of the chapel. On one side hung a four-foot reproduction of Jesus, his right hand knocking at a vine-framed door. On the opposite wall hung an oil painting depicting a sturdy lighthouse sending a beacon into a storm-tossed sea.

The front rows were occupied by a staff of thirty men being helped by the mission to put their lives back together. They did the practical chores: cooking, housekeeping, and maintenance, including buffing the gray vinyl floor to a high gloss. On each of 150 dark brown metal folding chairs, a hymnal awaited an occupant. Some staff chatted; a few were laughing. The street people waited in silence.

A homemade podium with a microphone occupied the center of the stage, and to one side sat a brown spinet piano. A lady sat down at the piano, opened the hymnal, and began to play softly. Brother Jim's voice intermingled with the sound of the piano as he instructed each person on the stage. "Brother Dan, pick out the songs the boys know--about three. You know which ones. Lucy, you gonna' sing one song, or two?"

Lucy was one of three women who came prepared to sing solos. "One," she said.

"You girls be sure to give your testimony before you sing. That'll help the boys." He didn't need to say much. He and his group had been following the same routine once a month for at least two decades. The pianist stopped playing when Jason, one of the staff, stepped up to the microphone.

Tall, light-complected with blond hair cut short, he barked into the microphone in the stern, no-nonsense voice of a drill sergeant. "There'll be no talking during the service. No littering. No spitting on the sidewalk outside. No sitting on the steps. Please stand only when asked to. Reading the Bible only is permitted. Showers and shaves on Monday and Thursday. Clothing is available, first-come, first served on Tuesday and Friday. Could we have two brothers, please?"

Two men from the staff rose, walked up to the altar, and bowed their heads. After a brief prayer, they turned to pass two small, woven baskets for donations, first on the stage among the guests, then among the audience.

As they disappeared at the rear of the chapel, Jason said, "Now, we'll turn the service over to Brother Jim and his group. Let's all give them a big hand."

A smattering of applause brought Brother Jim to his feet with a smile. During the years he had been coming to the mission, Brother Jim's hair had turned from black to salt and pepper. Other than that, not much had changed. His dusty black shoes and white socks were those of a working man. He removed a loose-fitting black topcoat that hung almost to his knees, revealing tan denim pants held up by a belt. His white dress shirt, open at the collar, was neat and clean, but not ministerial.

He announced with a smile, "We're here to praise the Lord, so get your hymnals and join in as Brother Don comes to lead the singin.'"

Brother Don opened his hymnal at the podium and the music began. The men sang with gusto familiar gospel hymns, "The Old Rugged Cross," "How Great Thou Art," and "When We All Get to Heaven," songs of hope and forgiveness with the promise of a better deal, if not here, then surely hereafter.

The soloists had background tapes of gospel music with a contemporary beat featuring a full orchestra and backup singers. The only missing part on the tapes was the solo, which the ladies provided. The soundman in the control booth at the rear had trouble managing the tapes. While he fumbled, the ladies shared their faith and expressed their love and concern for the men and their unfortunate circumstances. The twang from the first singer suggested an untrained voice; the other women's voices were more musical. The audience gave no sign they had noticed a difference.

After the last solo, Brother Jim came to the podium and presided as volunteers told what God had done for them, a privilege restricted to the staff and those seated on the stage. "Wine testimonies" from street people who might have had too much to drink were discouraged because they often dragged on and usually included things nobody wanted to listen to.

Finally, Brother Jim placed his well-worn King James Version of the Bible on the podium, opened it, and read. "All have sinned and come short of the glory of God." As he continued to read, he mispronounced difficult Biblical names and often missed words of three or more syllables. His torturous reading was immaterial; he had a message to deliver. He prayed, "God, anoint me to deliver the message you have for the boys here tonight."

He continued, "I left home when I was 14 and made a promise I'd never cry again," a vow he did not explain. "I drifted around, rode the rails, fought overseas, and drunk anything that come in a bottle or a can. I could swear with the best of 'em, and I done a lot of things I'm ashamed of, praise God. I'd fight at the drop of a hat just for the pleasure of seein' someone laid out with a broken nose, praise God." He had drifted for years with little to show for it.

He understood how the boys felt. "I know what you're goin' through, praise God, but," and this line he had repeated word for word, many times for many years, "what He's done for me, He'll do for you, praise God."

Then he came to the point in his sermon that he relished. He proudly pointed to his wife, Verleen, seated behind him on the stage. Verleen had never been a beauty, nor had he been handsome, but their union lifted him out of a life where he couldn't be himself, thinking he had to be tough. With her at his side, he had roots, someone to come home to, someone to share his life with.

He had often wondered but never understood why she consented to marry him. He was grateful he didn't have to put on a show for her, didn't have to hide his pain. She was the only person in the world other than himself he had ever loved or cared for.

As close as they were, their marriage hadn't affected his lifestyle. People at work still got out of his way when they saw him coming. His language still came hot off the grill, smothered in profanity. He still kept up with the best drinkers.

———

When Verleen's health began to fail, there was never any question about who would care for her. "Verleen had three major surgeries," he said. "We was in debt for medicine, hospitals, and doctors, praise God, and our bills was piled up knee-deep on the table. Just tryin' to keep bare essentials was real hard.

"Just about the time we thought we was through with our run of bad luck, Verleen got severe ep'lepsy. But I stayed in there. It was years went by and doctors come and went, one after another. They all finally give up. The pain medicines didn't work no more, and Verleen spent many a day and night in agony.

"I worked all day, then spent evenin's cookin', ironin', cleanin', and carin' for Verleen. Over three years," he continued, "she was nearly a total invalid, praise God. A few times she'd have a meal for me when I come home from work, but I never expected it, and she never done any more than that.

"One Tuesday they called work to tell me to come home, 'cause Verleen was havin' such a hard time. When I got home, the doctor was just leavin'. He said he couldn' help her, and he knew nothin' else to do, praise God. Verleen couldn' stop cryin'. I did what I could to comfort her, but that didn't help. I didn't know nothin' else to do, so I got busy with the housework. I thought it might take my mind off her suffering.

"Late that night I was all tuckered out. I set down in our ol' beat-up rocker. It tilted a little to the left, but I never had time to fix it. My mind was spinnin' like I was drunk. Verleen was so sick and in pain, it made my heart ache. It looked like we'd never get our bills paid. I was mad at the world and tired of livin'. All them things was whirlin' around in my head like witches dancin' around a pot of poison.

"I switched on the TV, lookin' for somethin', anythin' that would drown out my troubles for a few minutes. A religious program come on, but I was too tired to switch channels. The preacher on the TV looked me straight in the eye and said, 'Friend, if you need healing, GOD CAN HEAL!'

"When he said that, I felt like I'd been hit with a telephone pole, praise God. I knew they was somethin' special about the man. He said, 'Friend, just come over here and put your hand on the TV. We're gonna pray for you now.'"

Brother Jim continued his story as a freight train came rumbling down the tracks behind the mission, shaking the building as boxcars passed, followed by several minutes of click-clack-click-clack. Brother Jim was undeterred; he merely raised his voice till the train had passed.

"I heard Verleen there in the next room, groanin' in pain with no relief in sight. Before I knew it, I was on my hands and knees, crawlin' toward the TV. For the first time since I grew up, praise God, I started cryin' and I couldn' stop. I put my hand on the TV and listened while the preacher prayed.

"In my heart, I was pleadin', 'God, if there's a God, if you heal my wife, I'll go to church. I'll be saved. I'll do anything you ask! Just heal my wife!'

"Then I heard a voice. It told me to go to Second and Thomas. I couldn' tell if it was only in my mind or out loud. I didn't know, and I didn't care. I walked into the bedroom and told Verleen what had just happened, and for the first time in months, she slept the whole night through without wakin' up once, praise God."

———————————————⌾———————————————

"The next day I asked the only man at work who had ever acted friendly to me if he knew anything about Second and Thomas.

"He smiled and said, 'That's the church I go to.'

"I gave him the surprise of his life by tellin' him, 'I'll see you there next Sunday.' All the rest of that week I couldn' stop thinkin' about that voice that told me to go to Second and Thomas.

"When Sunday come, I had a time gettin' Verleen out of bed to dress her. At first, she couldn' stop tremblin'. When she finally stopped, she was as limp as a rag doll. Her arms flopped around and never went where they was supposed to. I told her, 'We're goin' to church.'

"When we pulled into the gravel parkin' lot at Second and Thomas, I didn't know what to expect. The little, white-framed buildin' looked like a garage.

"I got Verleen out of the car and through the front door. It was the first church I'd ever been inside in my life. They had rows of homemade benches, all facin' a stage at the other end of the room. A speaker's stand had a white cross painted on it. The preacher was preachin' up a storm. Nobody even looked up when we come in.

"I didn't know how to act in church, so I headed for the preacher. Verleen was limpin', and I was her crutch.

"When we got down to the altar, the preacher stopped right in the middle of his sermon. Ever'body was lookin' at us.

"He said, 'What do you want?'

"I told him, 'My wife is sick. I want you to pray for her to be healed.'

"The preacher said, 'Do you believe?'

"I said, 'If I didn't, I wouldn' be here.'

"He called for all the people who believed to gather 'round to pray for Verleen.

Them people was prayer warriors! They was used to spiritual battle! They swarmed the altar like a bunch of bees and began prayin' all at once. In a few seconds, the noise was almost deaf'nin', people cryin', beggin' for mercy, askin' for healin', confessin' their sins, demandin' that God heal Verleen.

Some of 'em was on their knees. Some had their hands in the air, some weepin', holdin' one another, placin' their hands on Verleen.

"I can't tell you how long it went on—an hour or two hours, I don't know. But it was like somebody give a signal. The prayin' stopped and a feelin' of peace fell over the room.

"Verleen lay before the altar as still as a baby in a crib, praise God. God had visited us. Verleen was healed. It was a miracle."

Brother Jim glowed. He had reached the climax of his story. "I can't describe the look on her face," Brother Jim said. Behind him, on the stage, Verleen's face showed only the marks of age and a long life.

He continued, "She looked at me like she couldn't believe what just happened. People was sayin', "Praise God! Praise God," and Verleen walked without help out to the car to go home.

"About a week later we went to see the doctor. He told us they wasn't no way medical science could explain what happened to her." Brother Jim took a deep breath and repeated his mantra: "And what He's done for me, he'll do for you!"

———— ⊶⊷ ————

As he descended from his emotional high, the glassy-eyed stares of the staff in the front rows made him break his rhythm.

What did that look mean? Didn't they believe him? Hadn't they been listening? He glanced first right then left, like an actor who had lost his place in the script searching for someone to cue him. Brother Jim's face had the blank, uncomprehending gaze of a shock victim. His head bent forward, looking toward the floor but not at it. He mumbled quietly, almost in an aside, "It's been a long time since anyone got healed at church. Now when someone's sick, they just say a little prayer, and ever'one goes home. No one wants to stay and pray it through."

Shaking his head, he lamented, "People just don't seem to have power like they used to. It's been years since I seen anybody healed."

God had not changed, nor His message. People were still sick and in need. Where were the miracles? Had he been wrong all these years? Would God do for these men what He had done for him and Verleen? And if God would, why hadn't He?

He suddenly felt like the singer who walks up a ramp to a raised platform. House lights dim, spotlights come on, and he is in his glory, singing the loud notes, the high notes, the long-held notes, and ending with "and the home of the brave!" That's the signal for the audience to finish the anthem with, "PLAY BALL!" The spots go off, and they shuttle the singer off the field. They have heard the anthem many times before, and the singer is instantly irrelevant. In a secret place, Brother Jim harbored the fear that as he finished his message, the men might stand up and shout, "LET'S EAT!"

Brother Jim's eyes glazed, his hands hung limp at his side, and his voice trailed off. "I don't understand . . . people aren't bein' healed like they used to."

Like a fish that had taken a hook but continued fighting, he plunged deep into his inner darkness. In those shadows, his persona welcomed him back to a familiar warmth and security. Almost like an afterthought, he offered, "God promises to heal if we believe . . . God always does what he says he'll do. If people aren't healed, I guess they just don't believe. It must be," he repeated, beginning to brighten up, "we just don't have faith like we used to, praise God."

He was back on script. "Now, anybody who wants prayer, come to the front and we'll pray for you." Still brighter with a smile and a vigorous nod, he repeated, "What He's done for me, He'll do for you, praise God."

The pianist began playing, "Just as I am, without one plea, O Lamb of God, I come." Brother Jim left the stage and stood at the altar with his arms outstretched toward the audience. Four men rose, one by one, and came to stand by him.

He talked with each one. Some men came off the stage and placed their arms around the shoulders of the four men. They all prayed aloud simultaneously while the audience waited patiently.

A s 8:30 neared, Brother Jim returned to the podium and announced over the microphone, "I see my time's about up. Anybody else who wants prayer, we'll meet you in the prayer room. Don't worry about supper. If you need prayer, they'll save some for you."

He bowed his head. "Dear Lord, thank you for the food these men are about to receive. Bless it to the nourishment of their bodies and bless the hands that prepared it."

Suddenly animated, 150 men came to their feet and filed out by rows, through a side door, down a long hall to a dining room where a hot meal awaited them. Brother Jim and his flock, clustering for protection, left by the same door they had entered an hour earlier. As the door closed behind them, two staff members began quietly straightening chairs for the next night's service.

Boone

On a bookshelf in a Goodwill thrift shop, a tiny book by Marc Gellman caught my eye, *Does God Have a Big Toe?* Based on Bible myths, it took me back to the year Mother died and I met God.

Mother didn't feel like opening Christmas gifts, but she enjoyed watching me open mine. The day after Christmas, she went to the hospital. When she came home in March, Dad had a bed for her in our living room. Because she was sick, Mrs. Blair came to help. She was old enough to be my grandmother, and I liked her a lot.

One day I got home from school, and Mom's bed was empty. Just like that. She was gone. Whenever my dad looked at me, tears came to his eyes, and he choked. It bothered me a lot. I wondered if I had done something wrong.

———— ∞ ————

After school was out, with time on my hands, I got permission from Mrs. Blair to hang out with Claude. He was 13, four years older than me. He knew I had no friends in the neighborhood, so he took me with him when he went to play baseball and let me play in the outfield.

On my way to Claude's, I came up behind an old man on the sidewalk carrying two sacks. He didn't seem very steady.

He halted, then went on again. When I got near him, one bag began to slip from his arms, and I caught it before it spilled.

"Thanks," he said. "You came along at the right time."

"That's okay," I said. "Where do you live?"

"Just across the street. I'll rest on this bench for a few minutes. I guess I bought too much," he said. His breathing was labored.

He asked me my name.

"Daniel, but everybody calls me Boone. What's your name?"

"My name is God." He said it just like you'd say, "My name is Henry," or "My name is George."

I never thought I'd meet God walking down the sidewalk in my neighborhood. I never thought about meeting God anywhere. "Do you mean God, like . . . in the Bible, or in church?"

"The same," he said.

I didn't know what to say, so I said nothing. When we reached his house, I placed the shopping bag on a table on his front porch. He didn't ask me in, and I wouldn't have gone in anyway. I knew about "stranger danger."

When I got to Claude's house, his mom said he was swimming at the "Y," so I headed back home. The old man was still on his front porch, asleep, I think.

As soon as I got home, I headed straight for the kitchen. I could smell the cookies Mrs. Blair was taking out of the oven. "Back so soon?" she said.

"Claude wasn't home. We have a new neighbor, an old man. He's in the house where the Norton's used to live. He said his name was God."

Mrs. Blair didn't think very long about that. She smiled and said, "Sounds like he might belong in some sort of home where people can look after him. What did he look like?"

"He's old, skinny. His clothes sagged. His hair's gray, sort of silver."

Mrs. Blair said, "He's probably got family who keep an eye on him."

———— ∞∞∞ ————

T he next day, on my way to Claude's, the old man waved, so I stopped to say hi. "I told Mrs. Blair you said your name was God. She wanted to know what you looked like."

"And who's Mrs. Blair?"

"She takes care of me while Dad's at work."

"Don't you have a mother?"

When I thought about Mother, I had a hard time not crying. I still missed her—in the morning, after school, at supper, at bedtime. I missed her in ways I had no words for.

"My mom had cancer."

"I'm sorry," he said.

I had to change the subject. "I told Mrs. Blair you didn't look like God."

"Really? And what does God look like?"

"I've seen a few pictures in books. You don't look like any of them."

"Does God look the same in all the pictures?"

"No. In one of them, God has an arm that looks like he's been working out. In all the pictures, he has lots more hair than you do."

He said, "Maybe the people who made the pictures were just guessing."

———— ❈ ————

L ater on, my dad and I drove past the Norton house, and there he sat. I smiled and waved, and he waved back. Dad pulled over, and we walked up to the porch. "Hi. I'm Boone's father. Welcome to the neighborhood. I understand you two met a couple of days ago."

"Yes. Boone was a great help. He's a good boy."

On the way home, Dad said, "He looks harmless enough, but don't be too friendly. Sometimes older people are unpredictable. Not because they're bad. They lose their self-control. Just don't bug him." Then he added, "You're right, son. He doesn't look like God to me, either."

———— ❈ ————

E ven though I couldn't match wits with the old man, the next day I gave it a shot. "How do I know you're God?"

"Why do you think I'm not?"

"You look old—but not that old," I said.

He said, "I thought we already agreed, you can't tell by looking."

I could have asked him to do some kind of miracle, I guess, but testing God didn't occur to me. At the time, hanging out with Claude was more important.

———— ❈ ————

T he last time I saw him at the Norton house, I talked about something I should have brought up the first time I met him, but I didn't. "My Sunday school teacher said when we get sick, if we pray, God makes us well. I prayed, and Mom didn't get well."

"Your teacher was close. I don't heal people, but when a person dies, I feel sad, like you and your dad. What kind of God would I be if I healed some people and skipped others? If you give me credit when someone gets well, you should blame me when someone doesn't."

"Did I cause my Mom to get sick?"

"You? You didn't make your mother sick any more than I did. You and I would never do that. Don't blame yourself for something you didn't cause."

"I thought I must have done something bad. My Sunday school teacher says when we're bad, bad things can happen to us. He says we ought to feel sorry and try to stop doing bad things."

"He's right. Feeling sorry can sometimes help us change."

So I asked him, "Do you ever feel sorry?"

"Oh, yes," he said. "I've felt sorry many times. A lot of people have suffered because of my mistakes."

It wasn't long before the Norton house was empty again. I didn't think about the old man anymore until one day I met Claude getting off the bus. He said he heard music at the bus stop downtown. There sat God on a folding stool, playing a violin. A few people were dropping money in his music case on the sidewalk. A couple of high school boys were laughing and making a lot of noise while their friend took money from his violin case. They all ran and jumped on the bus.

"Did you try to stop them?

"No. I didn't want to get beat up."

"Are you sure it was God?"

"I could tell. He figured out I was your friend. I told him I saw the boys and asked him why he didn't yell for the cops. He said he knew what they were doing. He said it's just stuff. It didn't bother him. But I talked to the cops who were nearby, and they talked to the old man but they didn't do anything."

Several weeks later I spotted an old man pushing a shopping cart along my street. He stopped to pick up a soda can. Seeing a violin case in his cart made me take a closer look. He needed a shave, and probably a bath, but it was him.

"God!" I said—was I talking to God, or swearing—"What happened?"

"Hi, Boone. I lost my house. I didn't have any place to go, so here I am." He didn't act depressed or anything. "I don't need much to get by," he said.

"How do you eat? Where do you sleep?"

"I get donations when I play my violin, and I collect enough cans to pay for lunch when I'm hungry. Poverello House serves breakfast and dinner, and they give out changes of clothes each week. They have beds, too, but on clear nights I sleep outdoors to enjoy the stars."

He was scuzzy, and I couldn't help looking.

"As for the dirt on my clothes and my hands, remember, Boone, I made the dirt, too." When I forgot he was God, a remark like that—about him making the dirt—brought me right back. He wasn't like anyone else I've ever known.

I haven't seen him since I met him that day on the street pushing a shopping cart, but when I see an old person picking up cans, I slow down, hoping to see a familiar face. The one thing I figured out about God is he's old. He's got to be old, right?

One Step for Man

O n Sunday morning, about midway on his cross-country trek, Kevin tossed his backpack into the bed of a pickup truck. He introduced himself to the driver, who asked, "Where you headed?"

"I've been hitching across the country, getting a close look at the 'real America.'"

"Well, son, you better spend a little time in this next village. It's off the beaten path, but I guess it's still part of America," he said and chuckled.

Keith stepped out of the truck and saw a village that reminded him of the small town where he grew up. Near its center stood a large church, the town's dominant feature. Keith strolled toward the building along with a steady stream of townspeople until he made out the church sign: Anabaptist.

A few cars dotted the parking lot, but most congregants were walking. Couples and families poured in through large open doors. An attractive young lady about Keith's age walked up the steps alone.

He thought she could have been a professional model with her strawberry blond hair and her figure. He quickened his pace to catch up with her but slowed when he noticed an older man and woman close behind her. The older woman was dabbing her eyes with a handkerchief she put away as she walked through the front door.

Keith followed them inside and watched the girl sit, straight and erect, with her chin high, the older couple just behind her. The older woman again dabbed her eyes. Into the pulpit strode a short, stout man, obviously, the pastor. He wore a tailored suit and had a gold cross hanging from his neck. He opened a Bible and read its majestic King James' English. The children sang, "I'll take my stand, where I know it's grand, on the B-i-b-l-e."

The sermon explained plainly to the congregation that they were sinners who needed salvation so their spirits may go to heaven when they die. Then, just before his benediction, the pastor reminded the people of a business meeting that evening.

At the close of the service, Keith strolled out to the church patio. A large coffee urn waited at the end of three long tables piled high with goodies, ranging from healthy snacks to some that might induce a diabetic shock. He watched the young lady get coffee and sit alone on a bench under a purple wisteria vine. The light green dress she wore complemented her hair and ivory skin tone.

He spread creamed cheese on a bagel, got coffee, and approached her. "May I join you?"

She glanced at Keith and said, "At your own risk."

"Wow!" he laughed. "What does that mean? What risk?"

"You must be the only person who doesn't know," she said, "if you don't."

Keith asked, "What's to know?" He gave her his brightest grin. "I'm Keith, Keith Larsen."

"I'm Daisy Thompson. The risk is that you'll be seen with me. The special meeting tonight is about me. It seems I've caused a bit of trouble. The meeting tonight will decide what to do about it."

"It sounds like a trial of some sort. You didn't rob a bank or something, did you?"

"No," she said. "It's not a long story. My philosophy professor asked our class, "What if Jesus never actually walked on water, as the book says?" I had heard that story countless times and never once considered whether it happened or not. When I asked the Pastor the same question, he turned red and was almost apoplectic.

"In our church," she went on, "we're trained from an early age not to question our beliefs. If someone questions, the church decides what's to be done. The most common outcome is to be 'churched.'"

"Being 'churched' is a bad thing?"

"Perhaps it should be called de-churching. It means that individuals are no longer a part of the community. They're shunned—even by their own family—and friendless. Eventually, those who are churched just sort of disappear, like my brother did."

"What happened to him?"

Daisy stood. "Look, I'll let my parents explain. It's Sunday, so you won't find any place in town open today. If you'd like to have dinner with us, Mother will set an extra place. My dad calls inviting a person to share a meal 'taking in the stranger within your gates.'"

"I'd love a home-cooked meal."

Keith fell into step beside Daisy. He glanced at the top of her head. She was only a few inches shorter than he was. When Keith saw their reflection in a store window, he thought, Not a bad-looking couple. This is a lady I'd like to know better.

D aisy's house, yellow with white trim, had a small front porch swing, built to glide, and a cushioned, wrought iron chair. As they entered through a screened door, Daisy's father pushed old-fashioned horn-rimmed glasses up on his nose and rose to greet them. "Daisy, what have we here?"

"Dad, this is Keith Larsen. I invited him to eat with us. Keith, this is my dad."

"Glad to meet you, Mr. Thompson. Thanks for your hospitality."

"Think nothing of it. We like company. Dinner will be ready soon."

Mrs. Thompson, graying hair only slightly out of place, came into the adjoining dining room wearing an apron over her church clothes. In her hands, she carried a place setting for their guest.

"Mom, this is Keith. Keith, my mom."

"Hi, Mrs. Thompson."

"Hello, Keith. We're glad to have you."

Daisy sat beside her father on a sofa upholstered with a print of large yellow and blue blossoms. Keith sank into a matching overstuffed chair.

"Daisy has me going, talking about being 'churched' and about your son. I'd like to hear more if you feel like talking about it."

"I wished someone would talk about it," he replied, pushing his glasses up on his nose. "People in our little town don't discuss this sort of thing." He leaned forward. "It's been hard on our family. When they churched our son Ricky, we handed over to the church all traces of him. We still have his junior high yearbook photo we found later beneath some other papers in the bureau drawer. We look at it and wonder where he might be today. Ricky and Daisy's cases are pretty much the same. Rick began asking a question here, a question there, back when he was Daisy's age. Then he was gone like a whirlwind."

"That just doesn't seem right to me," said Keith softly.

"It shouldn't have caught me off guard, but it did. I didn't know what to do. I felt sort of paralyzed," said Mr. Thompson. "It still hurts. Probably always will. We just hope he's okay."

Keith glanced up to see Mrs. Thompson staring at her husband with a look Keith could not quite make out. *Was it contempt? Or disdain? Or even revulsion?*

The meal was the best Keith had eaten in a long time: fried chicken, creamed gravy, mashed potatoes, his favorites. When it ended with cherry pie, Daisy began clearing the table and Mr. and Mrs. Thompson sat down in the living room. Keith remained standing.

"Mr. Thompson, thanks for your hospitality, and to you, Mrs. Thompson, fantastic food! Reminds me of Mom's cooking. However, if I'm not being too rude," he said, "I think I'll stroll up to the church and meet your pastor. My curiosity is getting the better of me."

Mr. Thompson looked up at Keith and said, "You're a stranger, but if there's any chance it might help, we'll appreciate it."

"At first glance, the situation seems unfair and unreasonable. I'd like to hear what the Pastor has to say about it."

Mrs. Thompson said, "The Pastor spends Sunday in his study, so you won't have trouble finding him. He tells us to rest on the Sabbath, but he doesn't."

⎯⎯⎯⎯⎯⎯ ∞∞∞ ⎯⎯⎯⎯⎯⎯

T he short walk back to the church brought Keith to a door marked "Office." A voice answered promptly: "Enter!"

Books lined the walls of the small space. The Pastor offered Keith a chair. "What can we do for you, young man? Keith, isn't it? I saw your visitor's card."

"Yes, sir, it's Keith. I had dinner with the Thompsons. They told me they had an older son whose case was similar to Daisy's. I've never heard of someone being 'churched.' What's that all about?"

"What's your interest in the matter, may I ask?"

"I think it boils down to curiosity. The Thompsons seem to me like the salt of the earth."

"Indeed, they are," said the Pastor. "And in times of crisis, our church's task is to preserve the salt. It's important to protect the community from outside influences. Daisy, sadly, appears to have slipped over the line. Nowadays, nothing is so insidious as the influence of college professors who seem determined to destroy their students' faith. We've been losing more and more of our young people."

Keith replied, "I still don't get it. Exactly what did Daisy do?"

"What she did was to question the Bible," he said.

"You mean about Jesus walking on water?" Keith said.

"Right. A strict belief in what the Bible says is essential. Any question with an uncertain answer discredits the entire book."

Keith thought for a minute. "So, your entire community hinges on a book? And more specifically, on your interpretation of the book?"

"There is only one interpretation. We cannot sustain ourselves if there are two possible answers. Questions would raise doubt." He paused. "May I offer you some cold water?"He poured two glasses and continued. "Let me guess, Keith, our church is not like the church in your hometown."

"It looks the same on the outside, but I've never heard of churching. I don't know what to make of it."

"Any question must be followed by its answer. It's a threat unless it is followed promptly by 'Yes, I believe Jesus *did* actually walk on water.' Daisy's question, you see, raises more questions. And to question the Bible is the same as questioning God." The Pastor concluded, "The outcome of our meeting tonight is almost a foregone conclusion."

Keith left, trying to piece together what he had heard. A very pretty girl who seems sensible, a good family about to have major surgery performed on it, and a church and its leader who live in a cocoon devoid of thought and feelings. None of it makes sense.

N othing in town was open except a 7-Eleven. The clerk, a young man about 20 years of age, greeted Keith with a friendly smile. "May I help you find something?"

"I'll take this soda and candy. By the way, how does it happen that you're open for business on a Sunday?"

"So travelers that need gas can get it and be on their way."

"I'm Keith."

"Fred. Most people call me Freddie."

Keith said, "Freddie, the thing that's happening at the church, Daisy, about to come under fire—what do you make of it?"

Freddie had a ready answer: "The church teaches us eternal truths. We never ask questions. Why question truth? There's no point in it, is there? Daisy stepped over the line, and the church can't ignore it."

Keith replied, "You're okay with what's going on?"

Freddie said, "Well, it bothers me, Daisy's getting cut out. I like Daisy and her family. We churched her older brother years ago." He shrugged. "Maybe there's something wrong with the whole family."

"Is it fair for her to lose everything in her life, her family, the community, and her friends, just for asking a simple question?"

Freddie said, "It depends on the question. If it questions the Bible, that's forbidden, so I'd have a hard time with that. But even so, you're right. That's a big loss just for asking a question."

"Freddie, tonight, shouldn't someone ask a question, not about the Bible, but about fairness, justice? What I'm saying is, shouldn't someone defend Daisy?"

Freddie frowned. "No one being churched has ever had a defense." His forehead creased as if he were trying to get it straight in his head. "My feelings for Daisy can't muddy my thinking, but I see your point. To be fair, someone should speak."

"Right," Keith said. "I feel like I've stepped into some sort of time warp." He looked out the front window of the store and said, "I think I'll take my snack over to the park."

⎯⎯⎯⎯⎯⎯⎯⎯⎯ ∞∞∞ ⎯⎯⎯⎯⎯⎯⎯⎯⎯

P icnic tables lined the back edge of a sunny, grassy area at the park. Keith sat in one of the swings, resting in full shade near a slide and a sandbox. By the time he had finished his candy and half the soda, he spied a woman approaching. It was Daisy's mother, coming straight toward him.

"Mrs. Thompson," he greeted her.

"Emma, please," she said. "I came to thank you for being interested in Daisy and our family. At times, I feel like no one cares. The rules are plain, and I don't think Daisy is sorry one minute that she's broken one. I can't think what to do. We've lost our son. I can't lose Daisy. I've grown tired of believing truth that has no heart."

Keith said, "Interesting phrase—'truth with no heart.' Is that what you're going to say tonight in Daisy's defense? I understand if no one speaks, whatever the members decide will go down without question."

Emma said, "That's the way it's always been. No one in town wants change. Mr. Thompson should speak up, but he's so busy being a Christian, if a tractor ran over him, he'd get up and apologize to the tractor."

"Why subject yourself to this? Why doesn't Daisy leave? We live in a big country."

"She hasn't said anything to us, but Daisy would never leave us voluntarily. We're her parents, and family is everything. But in our community, the church comes before family," Emma explained.

Keith looked at Emma and thought, *This little lady is no more than five feet tall, but I think that's no measure of her stature. I'm seeing the old adage in the flesh: "Don't get between a mother bear and her cub."*

He said, "Do you think there might be others who have doubts as you do but lack the courage to speak up?"

She said, "There must be. Other families have lost sons and daughters, or even a parent. Surely, we're not all unfeeling creatures."

Keith watched Emma walk away while he wondered what, if anything, he could achieve by getting mixed up in a matter that was none of his business.

That evening as Keith approached the church, the people gathered, most walking, as they had in the morning. The pastor stood near the entrance, greeting those who arrived early.

"Keith, my boy," he said, "all this must be a bit strange to you. I hope you're not disappointed by our action this evening. It's all for the good of the community."

They entered together, Keith turning to take a seat halfway to the front and the Pastor continuing up to the podium. Keith spotted Daisy and the Thompsons. Freddie sat alone.

"We'll come to order and declare ourselves to be in session. We have only one item to consider tonight. Sam, chairman of our Board of Deacons, will read the charge."

A tall, lean man dressed in a gray suit rose slowly, holding a paper in his hand. Keith suspected the Pastor may have written the note. Sam read, "As the Bible tells us, 'There is one faith, one baptism, and one body.' Daisy Thompson has questioned the Bible. We must declare her out of fellowship with this body."

The Pastor turned toward Daisy.

"Daisy, our sister, you have heard the report. Do you have anything to add, or is there any error in what Brother Sam has read?"

Daisy shook her head.

A pause followed, then the Pastor said, "All we need now is a motion and a second."

Sam said, "I so move."

For a while, no one spoke. The Pastor raised an eyebrow, and his eyes scanned the congregation.

Finally, came a voice, "I second the motion."

"We have a motion and a second. All in favor . . . "

Out of nowhere came a young voice. "Aren't we supposed to have a discussion before a vote?"

Like the crack of a whip, every head in the room turned, searching for the source of the statement. The Pastor's gaze swept the congregation like a searchlight. His scowl fell on Freddie. "Freddie, of course, you're right," he conceded. "Is there anyone who would like to speak?"

For a few seconds, no one rose. Then slowly and deliberately, Emma Thompson stood to her full height, her face like stone, determined, angry. She clutched the pew in front of her. "Everyone here knows our family, Mr. Thompson, me, Daisy, and our son Ricky who was churched years ago. Not a person here can accuse us of being bad people. Yet the church is about to do something bad to us. Now, it's my turn to ask a question. Why are you doing this to us?" She waited. "And I'm not going anywhere until I have an answer."

A murmur passed through the room. "The explanation is simple, Emma," the Pastor said.

A young voice interrupted. It was Freddie again. "Can a moderator take sides? He has to be neutral and see that each side has its say, doesn't he?"

"I suppose that's true, Freddie," the Pastor admitted, looking away with pursed lips. "Perhaps the Chairman of the Board can explain. Sam?"

Sam stood, staring blankly at the congregation, and said, "We've never had a divided congregation before. There's never been a discussion," and sat back down.

Freddie stood slowly and raised his right hand. The pastor said, "Yes, Freddie. You have something to say?"

Freddie turned, making eye contact with the group. "We all know the Thompsons are good people, not troublemakers. Daisy never said that she didn't believe. She only asked a simple question. Why can't she have an answer and we all get on with our lives?"

Across the room, a middle-aged man stood abruptly and spoke in clipped tones. "When my son was churched, there was no discussion. Nobody had to figure out anything—and we took it. He broke the rules. End of discussion. How's this any different? Why are we dickering about this now?"

Sounds of approval hummed across the room.

Emma rose again, turned to the man, and said, "Frank, have you completely forgotten Brian?"

Frank's face twisted in pain at the mention of his son's name.

Emma continued, "Have you erased all traces of Brian from your memory? What a good boy he was, loved by everyone in this room. And when he was wrenched from your arms, do you remember how you felt, seeing him walk out of this hall for the last time?"

Frank's shoulders began to shake, and he sobbed. "I'll never forget it! Day or night! God, forgive me!" Frank crumpled back into his seat, and the woman next to him put her arms around his shoulders. Several people around the room moved as if ready to stand and speak. The pastor dashed to the pulpit and grabbed the microphone. "Folks! Folks! Let's not let this get out of hand. We must come to order!"

The chatter continued unabated, so he finally shouted, "This meeting is adjourned! We'll come back Wednesday night and discuss this in an orderly fashion. You're dismissed." He darted out through a door behind the pulpit, and in a few seconds, the lights in the room began to go out one by one.

———⌘———

F reddie came up to Keith in the parking lot. "Keith, there's no place in town for you to stay. You can crash on my sofa if you like."

The light Freddie switched on in a small apartment a short distance away revealed a sparsely furnished living room. Leading the way in, Freddie said, "I'm gonna make some coffee. You want some?"

"Sounds good," answered Keith.

Freddie measured water in a carafe and spooned ground coffee into the machine. A red light indicated the brewing was in progress. "How do you take your coffee?"

"Black, thanks," said Keith. "It smells good."

He said, "Freddie, when you spoke up tonight, you set all this in motion. Is that what you expected?"

"I had no idea. I just felt like Daisy was getting railroaded. No one else would have said a word," Freddie said. "I wasn't even sure her folks would speak, but her mother said just the right things. I sometimes think women have more guts than men."

"Daisy hasn't said a word in her defense," said Keith. "Why do you think she hasn't?"

"Daisy needs no defense in my book. She's the prettiest, smartest girl in town. Most of the guys are afraid to go after her. I would but I don't have much to offer. Why would she give a second thought to a clerk? Plus, she's a year older than me."

"Maybe you're underestimating yourself," Keith said. "What you did tonight ought to earn you a few points with her. I like her self-confidence. She warned me not to speak to her after church this morning. She said I'd be taking a risk, like she was contagious. What do you think, Freddie? Are you in trouble, speaking up as you did? I think you upset the pastor. I'm guessing you may now be a target."

Freddie reached into a small closet and tossed a sheet and blanket to Keith. "Not necessarily. I didn't question what we believe—just how we were dealing with it." A yawn and a smile, and Freddie was off to bed. After struggling to get comfortable on the tiny sofa, Keith finally dozed off and slept soundly.

When he awoke, Keith could smell coffee. Freddie had left a spoon and bowl beside a box of cereal, clearly inviting Keith to have breakfast on him.

Sitting at the table downing his cereal, Keith scanned the apartment. Freddie was right. He didn't have much to offer a girl like Daisy. On the other hand, he had supported her publicly.

Keith walked to the 7-Eleven store to thank Freddie for his hospitality, but he was busy with customers, so Keith continued toward the church across the empty parking lot. He entered the unlocked building and continued to the office in the rear.

He heard the pastor's voice and paused. Whether the Pastor was praying, on the phone, or with someone in his study, Keith didn't want to eavesdrop. When the sound stopped, Keith knocked on the door.

"Enter," came the same friendly voice and tone as before. Keith greeted the pastor, who had been alone in the office, and took the offered seat. "Sir, I still don't know what to make of this church and this town."

The pastor responded, "This little problem is just a bump in the road. Our community is too deeply committed to entertain any possibility of change." He paused and frowned. "Make no mistake, anything less than churching Daisy would constitute a monumental shift." The pastor's pursed lips and creased brow suggested he was not so sure of the outcome as he sounded.

K eith had to know whether the people would throw Daisy out, so Keith decided to stay through Wednesday. He returned to the 7-Eleven, where Freddie was idle for the moment. "Freddie, I need a place to crash for a couple of nights. How about my using your sofa, and I'll buy a few groceries?"

"Great, I'd enjoy the company if you can stand the sofa."

When Freddie came home that night, Keith said, "What's the history of this little town? Has it always been like it is now?"

"Here's the short version of what I learned when I was a kid," said Freddie. "In the late 1800s, because of persecution, a small group of our ancestors emigrated from what is now western Russia and established this village. They set up this town off the beaten path to be free of worldly influences. Since then, every time any outside thought or idea comes this way, we quash it. Most of our members would choose to send Daisy away rather than risk contamination from a sinful world where doubt is acceptable. The pastor has told us numerous times that the words 'question' and 'heretic' have the same root meanings. And both lead to evil ends."

When Freddie left for work Wednesday morning, he told Keith, "I'm going straight to the church after work. You entertain yourself, and I'll see you there."

T hat night, when Keith neared the church, he noticed Freddie at the entrance, as if he were waiting for someone. Soon the Thompson's arrived with Daisy lagging behind. After Freddie had spoken on her behalf, Keith guessed she would speak to Freddie. Keith arrived at the entrance in time to hear the end of her sentence, " . . . if it hadn't been for you." She placed her hand on Freddie's arm.

Freddie blushed. He placed his hand over hers. "I think a lot of you, Daisy." He seemed unable to continue.

Keith followed them inside and stood at the back. He felt like he was observing a battleground where a great struggle was about to begin. Those huddled on his left spoke in somber tones, heads nodding. Those on his right were quiet, as if they had no leader, no one to rally them.

Daisy was alone in the second row from the pulpit, on the right, but apart from everyone else. The pastor's eyes canvassed the room as if looking for potential hot spots.

Keith wondered, *Who will stand up for Daisy? She can't defend herself. Emma already spoke. Freddie might, but it would be the voice of a boy, not yet a man.*

Seeing no one who might be Daisy's champion, Keith wondered, *Should I speak? I'm not even a member.*

"Let's come to order," said the pastor. "Let's be in order," he repeated. "We have one item to consider tonight. There has already been a motion and a second. We will give time for discussion, then we'll vote. Does anyone wish to speak?"

From the group, on Keith's left, a man stood. Keith recognized Brian's father, who had broken down weeping Sunday night. With a small note in his right hand, he composed himself and began to speak to the other side of the auditorium.

"I fell apart last Sunday when Emma Thompson mentioned my boy's name. I apologize. According to our rules, he was treated fairly, just like others before him. To hold together as a unit, we've got to stop all speculation and questions. If someone leaves, we weep for them, but we go on. We don't change. I'm sorry Daisy is taking the path that leads away from us. If she must leave, it's her choice. No one's forcing her to question the Bible. This is a bitter pill we've taken before, and we must do it again."

With a relieved look on his face, the pastor spoke, "Is there anyone else who would like to speak?"

To Keith, the silence seemed to go on forever. Then he noticed some movement among those on his right. Rising slowly, pushing his horn-rimmed glasses back in place, Mr. Thompson stood. Emma's eyes swept up to his countenance.

Of all people, thought Keith, *he's no knight in shining armor. He looks more like Oliver Twist with his hands outstretched begging, "Could I have more, please?"*

At first, Mr. Thompson spoke so softly that people leaned forward to catch what he was saying. "Friends," he said, "all of you know me. I'm not much of a talker. Standing up here is about the hardest thing I've ever done."

After a long pause, he continued in a louder voice, "You know I love our church. I would gladly suffer for you if need be. If I've offended anyone, speak now so I can beg forgiveness before I go on." He paused again.

"I love every person in this room, but above all, I love my family. When our son Ricky vanished, I felt like a wrecking ball flattened me. I still haven't recovered. Some of you have suffered in the same way. I don't think I can bear losing our Daisy. For what? What's she done? Has she hurt one of us? No. Has she said something that's untrue? No. Has she been unfaithful to our church and community? No.

"All she did was ask a question. In the Bible, people asked the Master questions. He didn't cast out a single one of them. Should asking a question bring down punishment on someone's head? Isn't it time for us to examine our practice of churching?"

"Sorry, Mr. Thompson," interrupted the Pastor firmly. "The motion is only about Daisy and her questioning the Bible. I have to rule you out of order."

From the other side of the room came a man's strong voice, "Let him speak!" followed by a soft "yes" from the people across the room.

And from the same voice, "We want to hear what he's got to say!" The pastor sat down almost as if he had been pushed.

Mr. Thompson went on. "I don't want us to fight, but we're already split, not by a bolt of lightning from heaven, but because our Daisy asked a question. Isn't the way we are treating Daisy as bad as the way outsiders behave? Isn't it time we make a change, and put an end to it? I say we should stop it—now."

Mrs. Thompson looked up at her husband. Struggling to hold back tears, she stood and embraced him. People around the room nodded in agreement.

The pastor almost leaped to the podium and reached below the rostrum. The microphone volume rose dramatically, and he shouted, "This meeting is out of order! I declare us adjourned till we can go home and consider the gravity of what Mr. Thompson's suggesting! Are we willing to risk all we have for one person? We'll settle this quietly and with dignity at our next meeting."

With that, he turned off the microphone and headed for the back where Keith figured the light switches must be.

F reddie fell in beside Daisy as the people disbursed. The pastor re-entered the darkened auditorium, heading for the exit.

"Pastor," Keith called out.

The Pastor squinted in the near darkness. "Keith? I never thought I'd see the day. I guess you know you witnessed something tonight that's never happened before in our community."

"Discussion and dissent?" asked Keith.

"Right," said the Pastor.

"Good luck," Keith said. "I'm taking off in the morning."

Surprised, the Pastor said, "Surely, you want some closure."

Keith smiled a gentle smile. "I'll admit I'm curious about the church, the Thompsons, Daisy, and even Freddie. But now, whatever happens, the people know they can speak freely. They can disagree, without fearing they've done something wrong. I think everyone grew a little tonight, including you, Pastor. It's a small step, but it's a step."

Grace, to You

The following is a translation of a Coptic manuscript by
Wayland Jackson, AB, BD, MDiv, BS. Overlooked by earlier
scholars, the manuscript, dating to the late first or early second
century of the Common Era, and penned to Grace, was found
in upper Egypt by Bedouins in 1948. According to academic
custom, the first words of the document are the official title.
Chapter and verse numbers have been assigned for use in
scholarly study.

Chapter 1

1 Grace, to you, and to Charity, and to all who hear the
words recorded in this book:

2 Being in the spirit on a Wednesday, I saw a vision of things
which are, but are not. [3]An angel of sorts spoke to me of
things visible and things invisible. [4]He was about four cubits
tall; his hair was beginning to turn gray, his clothing shone
like the noonday sun. He was wearing Nikes.

5 When I saw the angel, I fell to my knees. I would have
fallen at his feet, but I wasn't sure how long he had been
wearing the Nikes with no socks.

6 Seven rings were on his right hand. Light from his eyes
was like rays you might expect from the eyes of a superhero.

[7]His voice was like the sound of many rushing waters, only a little slower.

8 He commanded me: Rise. Come. Write these words about things that your eyes have never seen before. [9]Do not worry about plagiarism. Most of what I tell you to write is in the public domain, although not visible to many.

10 Write to the seven nations and to their seven rulers, arranged in order of their Gross Domestic Product, number five being California.

11 Blessed are they that hear the words of this revelation and mull over them, for the time is far gone, and we could use a lot more mulling.

C hapter 2

1 I asked the Spirit, What is this great thing you are going to show me? [2]The Spirit said, I will show you a city on a hill which cannot be measured. Like all cities set on a hill, it has twelve foundations and is walled.

3 There are twelve gates in the walls, three gates on each of its four sides: east, north, south, and west, arranged alphabetically and hypothetically.

4 The Spirit said to me, In the event you don't understand threes and fours, sevens and twelves, go to your local library. [5]Check out a book on numerology.

6 As a start, imagine the number three. That's an exalted oration, high, lofty, with three points. Four is the mundane: earth's four corners, four directions, four winds. Three and four added together become seven and multiplied become twelve. [7]Therefore, seven and twelve are complete numbers, the exalted and the mundane in union, like in a marriage, not like the AFL/CIO.

8 I will show you many things, the Spirit said. When we have exhausted the number of metaphors, count the things I have shown you. Insert the number here ___.

9 Then the Spirit led me through a deep chasm. I looked up and beheld immense walls that reached to the heavens.

10 It was a great city, bigger than Chicago.

C hapter 3

1 I saw twelve huge gates, actually only the three on my side of the great city; but based on what the Spirit said and simple logic, I assumed the other nine. [2]The gates I beheld looked like your average bejeweled gates, and the double doors looked as secure as the vaults at Fort Knox.

3 The Spirit said, The gates before you are ordinary, with one major exception. They are one-way gates. [4]You may enter by the gates but, once in, I just dare you to try to find your way out. [5]Nevertheless, said the Spirit, it can be done, and it has been done by a few.

6 I beheld a couple of people, wandering aimlessly outside the walls.

7 Spirit, Who are these outside the wall, and what are they called? [8]They are called the Select. Unlike the Elect who live in the city, the Select live outside the wall. They are not homeless, but they are city-less. [9]They live less in the urbs and more in the sub-urbs. [10]Oh, I said, not really understanding.

11 The Spirit said, From inside, the walls are invisible. The Select who live in sub-urbs found, by experiment or by accident, that the walls of the city are permeable. [12]Although, from the outside, the walls seem to be insurmountable.

13 Once inside people are not aware that they are walled in. [14]They may leave their square or leave the city at any time, but the doors only open to seekers.

15 The Select came through the doors unhindered and without injury. [16]They feel no urgency to persuade those inside the city to join them.

17 What good would it do? they ask. None, they tell themselves. [18]If their former friends are happy, what's the point? said the Spirit.

Chapter 4

1 I said, Spirit, what will you show me first? ²First, said the Spirit, we must enter the city. ³I said, How shall we open the great door, seeing we have no key? ⁴The Spirit said, Not to worry. The doors are not locked. However, every gate has its own entry ritual. ⁵Come, I will show you what's behind door number one.

6 Door One had a steeple above it with a thousand tiny silver bells that hung in great clusters like grapes. ⁷As we approached, the doors swung open, and the bells tingled, raising peals of joy that echoed across the city.

8 The Spirit said, Entering the city involves a gatekeeper and water. ⁹I get it, I said. The gatekeeper is like a butler or a tour guide—but teach me about the water.

10 The water is real, said the Spirit. You are going to get wet, very wet, or maybe only a little, but wet you will get.

11 I asked, And what is the purpose of the water? ¹²The Spirit said, Water is a great symbol. ¹³It is essential to sustain life. Remember to hydrate. It is useful for cleaning both hands and laundry. It's also an extender. If you have food for twelve, but thirteen guests show up, add water

14 Today you get the deluxe treatment, said the Spirit. ¹⁵Suddenly, as if I were on a conveyor belt, I began to move forward. ¹⁶I heard many machines. ¹⁷Brushes swirled, soap splatted on me, and was rinsed off. ¹⁸But at the end, no one sopped up the excess water or wiped my glasses. ¹⁹I drip-dried as our journey continued.

Chapter 5

1 Before me, a great city that no man can measure was laid out like a gigantic grid, with perfect squares, separated by gray streets to the right, to the left, and straight ahead. ²Each square held a multitude of people.

3 The Spirit said, Pulses from the center of the great city roll over the city and its inhabitants regularly. ⁴They all feel better after a good pulse. ⁵The pulses are pulses

of affirmation. "Yes, you are right," the pulses say. "You're superior." "Your life has meaning." "You're the ideal." [6]But we must see other things first.

7 Spirit, I said, the gray roads that separate the squares look odd, but the inhabitants inside the squares look normal. The [8]Spirit answered, What did you expect? In a vision, something must relate to the real world, or it will get too fantasmagorical.

9 I said, I see bistros around each square with people seated on sidewalks, eating, drinking, and laughing. [10]But all the patrons' backs are turned to the gray way that separates them from other squares. What's up with that?

11 The backs of the people form a wall. [12]Walls keep things out. Walls keep things in. [13]You can't wall someone out without walling yourself in. The bars on your neighbor's windows work both ways.

14 I asked the Spirit, Why are the gray streets almost deserted? Don't the groups have intercourse? [15]Spirit replied, Don't get cute with your little double entendres. And don't say, Look it up.

16 Behold those two trying to talk across squares. Their words are both audible and visible. [17]Notice that the words of one fly over the head of the other, and vice versa. They talk over each other's heads, not to each other.

18 The head of each block maintains that other blocks are dangerous. "Patrons in other blocks," he tells them, "are different." [19]They look the same on the outside, but their minds are disoriented." [20]The Block Head says, "People in other squares cannot tell north from south, nor up from down, like we can." For the most part, people in his square believe what the Block Head tells them.

21 A few may be pushed, jump, or fall into the gray area, or be set adrift, fly, or vault into another square. [22]Those who move to a different square can look back and see the square they have left, completely unaware that they are still in a square, just a different square.

Chapter 6

1 Let's move on, said the Spirit.

2 Inside one square, I beheld a building that reached up to the clouds. Yes, there were clouds—regular, fluffy clouds. [3]Across the building entrance was emblazoned the word: BROKERAGE. [4]I asked the Spirit, What's the purpose of a brokerage in the walled city? [5]The Spirit said, What do you think? Everything runs on money.

6 He said, Think infrastructure. Even a street of gold gets potholes. Every million years or so, a fire breaks out, and they deal with it.

7 But, I said to the Spirit, if this is heaven, what is the need of a brokerage, or money of any kind? [8]Heaven? said the Spirit. Who said this is heaven? This revelation is of things you see every day that are invisible to the eye.

9 The Brokerage is a reminder that while money is not the wheel, it is the grease. [10]And if you want to grease someone's wheels, green is best, depending on the kind of currency you're using.

11 I said to the Spirit, What a great mystery. In a visionary world, I would never have expected the inhabitants to use currency, green, or any other color. [12]The Spirit said, Don't be daft. The color is irrelevant. The wheels they grease are real and not real. [13]They are real in a pump, sucking oil from the earth, but almost completely invisible in the halls of power.

Chapter 7

1 The facade of the next great building bore in large block letters the word: EDUFACE. [2]What is this mystery? I asked the Spirit. [3]The Spirit said, EDUFACE is the education center. [4]When a person steps inside a square, the word on the building looks like EDUCATION. But when one looks across into a neighboring square, one sees EDUFACE and knows his square is superior.

5 So, I said, are the people still learning literature, science, and the arts? [6]No, answered the Spirit. That would be

education. EDUFACE is not a misspelling. It's education—in your face. [7]So, Spirit, is there education or is there not? [8]Loosely speaking, yes; actually, no. Indoctrination is more accurately what they do, said the Spirit.

9 Each block has its own ways, its own facts, its own prejudices, its own fears. [10]The job of EDUFACE is to perpetuate the mores of the people in its square, to inculcate their facts and prejudices, and to perpetuate their fears.

11 Once a person gets inside a square, what is done there will seem right and true to him—or to her, to be inclusive.

12 I said, That doesn't sound like any kind of education I've ever encountered. [13]It's all in the viewpoint, the Spirit answered.

14 So, Spirit, is the purpose of education to keep people in their squares? [15] The Spirit said, Not only to keep them in but also to entertain them. [16] Spirit, that sounds to me like Fantasyland. [17] The Spirit corrected me, Disney engineers on their best day could not have imagined this walled city.

C hapter 8

1 I said to the Spirit. Do I understand correctly? [2]Each square is a world of its own? Its inhabitants do not question its values or ethics and view all other squares as somehow inferior? [3]The Spirit said, Yes. The people of each square think they are the Elect. [4]They do not question themselves or their own lives.

5 The major fear in every square of the walled city is fear of self. Second, like unto that is fear of someone who is different. [6]The people are taught, and they believe, that the gray areas that separate them are fraught with uncertainty and danger, and they are not entirely wrong.

7 Oh, I said, 'gray areas' is a metaphor. [8]Correct, but not a very good one if it must be explained.

9 Is there more you want to show me?

C hapter 9

1 The Spirit said, The city set on a hill is ruled by a great one, not visible to the eyes. But he's there, or she is, or whatever. I cannot say for sure. [2]I said, Do you mean like the Wizard of Oz, a great one whose voice is heard but whose countenance no one has ever looked upon? [3]The Spirit said, Don't be simple. Everyone has seen the Great One in the Wizard of Oz if you've ever watched Turner Classic Movies. It's all a trick.

4 I said to the Spirit, Then, is God the ruler over the great walled city? [5]No, said the Spirit. The ruler is called the Nameless One, or One with a Thousand Names.

6 Doesn't that make him, her, or it, God? I asked. [7]You can call her, him, or it, God, if you wish. That doesn't make it God, just as you can call this place heaven, but that doesn't make it heaven. For all I know, it's hell.

8 Hell? I said. How can that be? The people seem happy. The chatter is endless. The squares seem lively.

9 Staying in one square, never venturing into gray areas, hearing the same message day after day is like eating the same food at every meal, said the Spirit.

10 Eating butter fudge chocolate brownies for a million days, even with a tall glass of cold milk, is anesthetizing.

11 In their hearts, they know there is more. [12]More what? I asked the Spirit. [13]More dessert, more of everything. Baklava, lemon meringue pie. A better menu. Freedom.

14 Spirit, I said, are the people like mountain climbers who reach a peak every day, then look ahead to discover only another horizon? [15]Cliché alert! Let's just stick with the walled city, said the Spirit.

C hapter 10

1 Spirit, I don't see any birds. Why is that? [2]I don't know. I like birds. I didn't decorate the place.

3 Does that mean we cannot get a bird's-eye view of the city? [4]Of course not. You don't have to stand in a tunnel to have tunnel vision.

5 Then, we soared to great heights, but not too high, because I get airsick. [6]I saw people sitting in a gigantic circle inside one square. No one spoke or moved.

7 Spirit, I said, Who's in that square? Are they calm, or are they dead?

8 Those are Quakers. They are dreaming of a world where thunder makes no sound. [9]You know their motto: In case of emergency, please be quiet.

10 And Spirit, the square over there is completely surrounded by shades.

11 The Spirit said, Correct. No one can see in or out. They're nudists. Shades keep outsiders from viewing all that flesh, and they protect insiders from the looks of horror and amusement on faces looking in.

12 I see a busy square, Spirit, people marching around, holding signs. A few have megaphones. [13]Those, said the Spirit, are protesters. Leaders are the ones holding megaphones. Something is always wrong, and they always feel a need to fix it. [14]They protest climate change, high taxes, clowns, the right to bear arms, government meddling.

15 See? said the Spirit. One protester has a sign protesting protesters. [16]It's a serious business. No one smiles, and no one fools around.

17 I said, A barber would have a field day in that square. Every man has a beard. [18]A barber would be out of business in that square, said the Spirit. Those are Sikhs. They never cut their hair. Something about their religion. [19]The Sikh square has one door on each side, just like the Golden Temple.

20 I see a square with polka dots on the floor and people going from one dot to another. Who are they? I asked. [21]They're historians. Each dot is a verifiable fact. They spend their days trying to connect the dots with theory thread. [22]They resemble the ancients who drew pictures by connecting stars in the sky, you know, a fish, a hunter, a big dipper. They saw the stars but lacked depth perception. [23]History buffs create pictures of a past that never was and never will be.

C hapter 11

1 Spirit, there's a square shaking like gelatin. [2]Everyone has sideburns, gyrating hips, and a microphone. [3]Those, said the Spirit, are Elvis impersonators.

4 Spirit, I see one square absolutely full of smoke. Let me guess who's in that one. [5]Spirit said, be my guesser. Ha, ha.

6 Those must be pot smokers, I said. They couldn't find a door if they wanted to. They can't even find a wall, can they? [7]Spirit said, They're not looking for a wall or a door. They're looking for a sofa.

8 Spirit, that square reminds me of an old TV ad in which apes tossed suitcases around their cage to test them. Can it be? [9]It can, he said. [10]Baggage handlers throw suitcases and bags, bouncing them off the walls, stomping on them. [11]Some of them rummage through the bags, Spirit said.

12 And who are the strange-looking people in that square? Their eyes are bugged out, a box rests on their chests, and they all have four arms. [13]Those are accordion players. After only a few minutes in there, everyone's eyes are buggy. They use the extra hands to stop their ears. [14]Those people think they are in hell. So, do I.

15 Whatever occurs to you, we have a square for it, said the Spirit: feminists, Sunnis, generals, Okies, popes, libertarians, Inuits, terrorists, lumberjacks, surgeons, [16]used car salespeople, the homeless, hospital orderlies, fighters (or pugnacionists), airline landing crews, and pilots of all sorts. There are bazillions of squares.

17 Bazillions?

18 Bazillions.

C hapter 12

1 You won't remember all the squares, said the Spirit, but let me give you a few to choose from when you write.

2 There is a nerd square. It requires a test of computer language and knowledge of connectors to get in.

3 The square with people pounding nails in, and pulling them out, and nailing them in again, is for handymen. Some are handywomen.

4 There are squares for pet lovers: lovers of dogs, cats, ponies, snakes—you name it.

5 There is a square for people pleasers who can't stop smiling. They just want everyone to like them.

6 The square with people dressed loudly wearing floppy shoes standing around a VW automobile is for clowns.

7 The people running amok are gun lovers. They take turns shooting and being shot at. No one ever gets hurt.

8 The square with a stage is for standup comics. They rate each other by holding up cards numbered from one to five.

9 Spirit, I said, who is that motley crew? They look so confused. [10]Those, said the spirit, are writers. See? They all have pens, paper, and laptops. Indeed, they are a motley crew.

11 What is this square next to them? People there also have pens, paper, and laptops, but they are drinking wine and eating cheese. Those, said the Spirit, are writers who have sold something. Ah, yes, I grimaced.

C hapter 13

1 Spirit, let me put some questions to you as we travel. [2]Fine, I can do questions, he said.

3 What if a person fits in more than one square? For instance, what if a person is a feminist as well as a terrorist?

4 Spirit joked, Aren't they the same things? Ha, ha, ha. Take my wife, please! I'm on a roll! [5]But seriously, the answer is that if a person has more than one label, one of the labels floats to the top, and that's where he goes. For instance, a person who is gay and likes drums might end up in a square with other gays, prioritizing his gay identity over his love of bongos. Next.

6 Why are some blocks more densely populated than others? [7]Because, some blocks are more densely populated than others. Next.

8 What things, I asked the Spirit, are common to all groups? [9]All have financial institutions and educational institutions.

They all have Heads—bosses I mean, not toilets. And they all shun.

10 Shun? I said. [11]Yes, shun. If an individual gets too far out of line, he or she is relabeled and shunned. [12]I asked the Spirit, How is a person shunned?

13 You get the "look," the message. One way or another you will leave the group, voluntarily or forcibly. [14]You might move to a more compatible group, or just wander around in gray areas. Or you might find the invisible gate in the invisible wall and go live in the sub-urbs.

15 It's like this, said the Spirit. Every group believes it has the truth by the big toe, when all it really has is a big toe. [16]It clings to its truth to justify its existence.

17 If they question themselves, it will only be in superficial ways. [18]Meaning what? I asked. [19]Well, for example, a doctor's group might debate the differences between saline solutions and sucrose solutions, but they would never question the importance of the heart as an organ. [20]Or, in another example, a religious group might argue about the best way to baptize, but it would never ask, Should we worship at all?

21 You see, said the Spirit, because all of them are *all right*—*all* of them are wrong. No one owns truth, not even God.

C hapter 14

1 Spirit, what is at the center of the city? If it is not like the Wizard of Oz, then what is it like, and who dwells there? [2]The Spirit moved us north, or was it west, toward the center. [3]Was it like California? I wondered.

4 The sound of mighty waters grew to an unspeakable roar. [5]Yes, I thought. This must be California. [6]No, said the Spirit, it's not California.

7 And don't get close to the center. [8]Those who do may be drawn into a hole. [9]It resembles a black hole, but it could be any color. [10]The point is this: once you start down the pike, there is no escape, no returning. [11]You will never be heard from or thought of again. So, don't get near it.

12 The main thing to remember is the noise. The center is full of noisy noise. [13]You'll not find a Quaker within a mile.

14 The Spirit added, This would be a good place to use one of my favorite words: cacophony. Look it up.

C hapter 15

1 I am puzzled, Spirit. ²Can you explain why I saw no jail or prison in any of the squares? ³Because each square is itself a jail, said the Spirit. The people are all prisoners of their own environment. A way out only *seems* to be a way out. ⁴The beings who have escaped and think they are superior have not gone much further than the sub-urbs.

5 Spirit, I notice the glaring absence of oriental or Near Eastern references. Why is that? ⁶That, said the Spirit, is because I am a Western spirit. In a way, I too am in a square. I have spent my life with my back turned to the East. ⁷At times, I feel like a madman in a straitjacket of Westernism.

8 I said, Spirit, given all the commonalities, the city still doesn't make sense. Where is the pattern? What unifies it? Where is the plot? ⁹The Spirit said, Those elements are all missing because this is life. Life is messy, not like a story, which is logical and orderly, with great dialog and sharply drawn characters. ¹⁰Life doesn't make sense, said the Spirit. It never has. Never will. ¹¹If you want to go to a place that makes sense, go to the bank. Ha, ha, ha—a little Spirit humor.

C hapter 16

1 Spirit, what gems of wisdom can I write that you have not yet revealed to me? ²The Spirit said, I apologize. I am all out of gems. ³Surely, Spirit, there must be something. We've come so far. ⁴And learned so little, said the Spirit. All right, he said, I'll give it a try.

5 No one knows, he said. ⁶No one knows—what? I asked. ⁷No one knows much compared to what there is to know.

Everyone is smart compared to when he or she was born, but overall, none of us knows much. [8]What can we learn from that? I asked. [9]He said, That 'none' takes a singular verb.

10 Sorry, Spirit, that won't cut it. That's not enough. [11]Spirit said, How about this? Even though we are *all* wrong, it's okay for everyone to think he or she is all right.

12 But Spirit, what if someone who thinks they're all right wants another to adopt his or her brand of 'all right?' [13]The Spirit said, I'm embarrassed to answer in this way, but that's life.

14 I will offer an observation, although observations are not my favorite things: [15]Every moment in a person's life is unique. Therefore, there can be no rule that always applies.

16 Spirit, I feel like a dog chasing its tail. Does life go in circles? [17]I don't do geometry, said the Spirit. I'll have to take a pass on that.

18 Then the Spirit brightened and said, How about this for a takeaway? Offer $5 to anyone who has read this to the end. Make it worthwhile to a few at least. [19]I said, I've only got $65. If thirteen people read this and ask for the $5, I will be flat broke. [20]Spirit said, Trust me. You're not going to run out of money.

21 It's my turn to ask a question, said the Spirit. The degrees of the translator listed at the beginning of this work, I understand all of them except the last one, BS. [22]You're kidding. You really don't know what BS is? Spirit, you're hopeless and I am sleepy and bone tired.

23 Instead of writing down all you have shown me, I think I'll just wait for the movie.

24 You disappoint me, said the Spirit.

25 That's life, I said.

Me and the Good Book

I began attending K Street Baptist Church in Ardmore, Oklahoma at age sixteen at the urging of my oldest brother and his wife. The church met in a newly constructed, white wooden building furnished with homemade pews. Every person in the congregation was encouraged to bring a Bible to church. The Bible was the center of every sermon.

In my mind's eye, I can still see Rev. Ross Hughes gripping the sides of the pulpit with both hands, bringing to life the story of Gideon and the Midianites. Gideon, instructed by God, was ordered to pare his army down to a small handful of men; then, to our great relief, with God's help, his small band routed the Midianite oppressors.

I "courted" the Bible. We were a couple, me and the Bible. True, God was everywhere, but the Bible was the heart of the matter. God and the Bible, like Siamese twins, were vitally connected. Everything I knew about God came from the Bible. The words I used to describe one worked equally well with the other. Both were holy and without error. In the Bible lay eternal life and truth, just like God.

During my days at Oklahoma Baptist University, I "married" the Bible—not a formal church wedding—more like a common-law marriage. "All scripture is inspired by God." (II

Timothy 3:16). To me, the logic was clear. All Scripture was inspired; the Bible is the Scripture; therefore, the Bible is the inspired word of God.

Billy Graham had just come on the scene. He was one of us. His devotion to the scriptures was a model for us. I felt confident we Baptists followed the Bible more closely than other Christians. We were the "people of God," loving our Bibles—the Word of God.

I was on automatic pilot to become a denominational hack, following the party line like a sheep. However, after a long marriage to the Bible, a breakup came—not overnight, but gradually, like the turning of an oil tanker. A pivotal step was my leaving the professional ministry at age 40. Outside denominational boundaries, I felt free to ask questions I would probably never have asked if I had stayed in the profession. Being an insider would have stifled inquiry.

An early wake-up call came when I discovered not a single original copy of any writing in the Bible exists today. We must make do with handmade copies, separated by centuries from the originals. Among the more than 5,000 manuscripts and pieces of manuscripts we now have, no two are identical. That means there is no single "Bible." There are 5,000 "Bibles" scholars comb in search of the original documents. Maybe those were inspired, but no living person has ever seen one.

Another turn came in a Presbyterian Bible study. I was secure in my view that the only way a human can relate to God, as delineated by Paul in Ephesians, is by faith. Humans cannot gain God's favor by simply living a good life. My view was challenged by the group's leader who suggested I read Jesus' account of the great judgment as told in Matthew.

In Matthew's story, the king separates the people as a shepherd separates sheep from goats. He invites one group to enter the kingdom, giving ,as His reason, they had cared for him.

Surprised, they asked, "When did we help you?"

The reply was, "When you did it to the least of these my brethren, you did it to me."

With no mention of grace, or faith, or even Jesus, I faced the possibility that Paul in Ephesians described one way into the kingdom; while Jesus, in the gospel of Matthew described another.

Encountering apparent contradictions, like Paul's message of salvation by faith alone versus James' message that "faith without works is dead," like all Baptists, I adopted Paul's view and rationalized James' view away.

I never thought I was worshipping the Bible, yet I used it as a representation of God, something most people would call an idol. I would hold the Bible in the air and begin a sermon with the words, "God said," as if the Bible were God.

If God wrote the Bible, I began to wonder why He used writers who were bad spellers and who used poor grammar and rhetoric. *Why did it take centuries to pull it together? Why not just deliver the finished product?*

Further, if an all-powerful God took the trouble to write the Bible, why didn't He also preserve the original copies, so there would be no question about what He said?

When I raised these questions in my favorite online chat room, they quickly and sternly rebuked me. The charge invariably was if I only "had the Spirit," and therefore "discernment," then I wouldn't be asking questions. They said, "Those who aren't Christians can't understand or accept the Bible because they are not taught by the Holy Spirit." Translation: If you don't interpret the Bible as I do, then you must not know God. To some in the chat room, my questioning was proof I was not a Christian. Ironically, the people who charged me with not having discernment seemed to have it in abundance.

Another change of direction in my life came when my men's Friday Bible group studied "Rescuing the Bible from Fundamentalism" by the renegade Episcopal Bishop John

Shelby Spong. Without endorsing any of his views, I felt encouraged to discover at least one other soul in the world besides me was asking questions.

Spong, as it turned out, was a member of the infamous Jesus Seminar who vaulted Biblical criticism into popular culture for a couple of decades. The Jesus Seminar produced its flagship book, "The Five Gospels," based on the assumption we can study scriptures from a historical standpoint.

M y attachment to the Bible was deeply rooted in my psyche. The thought of ending my "marriage" to the Bible brought a torrent of questions. *If I divorced the Bible, would I still be a Christian? Would other Christians shun me? Should I abandon the Bible altogether? Had I lost my faith? Was there a place where I might discuss my feelings? Would I sit in judgment of friends who were unwilling or unable to ask similar questions? Were they idolaters? Could we even discuss it?*

The idea that God is everywhere and therefore ever-present had long sat undisturbed in my mind. When I least expected it, it quietly slipped over the threshold and dropped into my heart. A light dawned. I "knew" God in a different way. The Bible was off the throne. God occupied it fully.

As I saw it, I had substituted a marriage certificate for marriage, a cookbook for a meal, an oil painting for a sunset. I had settled for Biblical descriptions of others' experiences of God without thinking of my own. But that was no longer necessary.

Attempting to describe my coming to know God, I coined the word *GodPresent*. However, explaining religious experiences is like trying to describe the taste of ice cream. For the person who has never tasted ice cream, no description is adequate. And the person who has tasted it needs no description.

A s for "Me and the Good Book," I enjoy what has been called a "friendly divorce." As part of my "divorce settlement," I abandoned the traditional doctrine of inspiration. Instead, I learned to read without filtering texts through my theological upbringing. I weaned myself from inserting, even subconsciously, words like 'literal,' 'inerrant' or 'authority.' I eliminated the use of phrases like "The Bible says . . ." or "It says . . ." in favor of "Leviticus says . . ." or "Paul wrote . . ." or some other phrase indicating the primary source.

To my surprise, as soon as I began to let the writings speak for themselves, studying the writings became a delight. The Bible is a remarkable collection of writings. I respect Biblical accounts of experiences of God, illustrated numerous times in Bible stories. I also respect records of experiences of God outside the Bible. I have equal respect for people who have had no experience of God nor any desire for such an experience.

The Trial

O ur children have graduated college and moved to the
    city, so it's just my wife Rose, and me. We live in a small
village settled by our ancestors who fled the Great Potato
Famine in the 1840s. They came to Rhode Island because it
was a state that tolerated Catholics. Our faith and customs
have remained the same over the years.

Each Sunday, Rose goes to mass; I go to The Boar's Head.
The two are similar in three ways. First, they both offer
fellowship with people of similar tastes. Then, you get a nip
of the old brew in both places—more than a nip at a bar. And,
if you believe God is everywhere, then He's at the bar just like
He's at mass. The wife and I get home about the same time
and spend the rest of the day together.

One Sunday, I asked her as usual, "How was mass?"

She said, "Mass is mass. Mass never changes. Everything we
did last week, we did again today. Everything we did today,
we'll do again next week. Everything the same at the pub?"

"Well, I'd say a little bit different."

"Oh?"

"A fight almost broke out."

"A fight? At the Boar's Head? For heaven's sake, Mickey,
what could you boys possibly fight about?"

"You're not gonna believe this. It was about God."

"God? A fight over God? In a bar?" She burst out laughing.

"Laugh if you want, but I'm not kidding."

"Did some Protestant sneak in and say something wrong?"

"No, it was Pat—Pat Robinson. He was hitting it pretty hard and started spouting off about the shape the world's in today, the homeless, the environment, corruption. He kept saying God was doing a shitty job. The whole bar could hear him. He went on and on, not blaspheming, but sort of insulting God.

"When he mentioned abusive priests, that ticked off some of the guys. We don't go to mass often, but we're still Catholics."

"So, why didn't you send him home in a taxi?"

"We tried, but he refused to leave. He kept hanging onto his drink and saying we should *do* something. Then his eyes got so big you'd think he'd seen the Virgin.

"'I got it!' he shouted. 'I say we put God on trial—for mismanagement and gross negligence.' Then he started blubbering. He wiped his eyes and his nose and got very serious. He said, 'Let's put God on trial.'

"Finelli said Pat was crazy. How could you put God on trial? First off, who's got the nerve to judge God? And where would we find a jury of His peers?

"Pat said we could have a trial without a jury. We only need a judge.

"But, Finelli kept on asking who would do that. Not an atheist, and a religious person wouldn't be impartial.

"Pat was drunk, but he thought for a moment and said, 'How about Marty?'

"He looked at Marty and back at us. We had to admit he's the best barkeep in Rhode Island, and he never takes sides. He'll be fair.

"Then, Marty jumped in and said, 'Hey. If this is about God, leave me out. I don't want to be in the middle of it. I've got enough troubles without that.'

"Pat was slurring a bit, but his mind was set. He said, 'No, Marty. You're the only one who can do it. You're fair. You look at both sides. We all trust you.'

"Marty said, 'You're asking me to run a trial with God on the dock? Are you joking?'

"Some of the guys shrugged like it was okay with them. A few brave souls said it might be fun.

"I told the boys that to shut Pat up we should agree, but I warned them to keep it quiet. If word gets out, we'll have Father Francis on our tails, and we'll be the laughingstock of the whole town."

Rose interrupted, "Excuse me, but it sounds to me like you all had too much to drink, and Pat's the worst of the lot. A bunch of silly old men."

The following Sunday, when she left for mass, Rose grinned and said, "Don't do anything I wouldn't do, like put God on trial." Then she waved as she drove away with a big smile on her face.

The parking lot at the bar had more cars than usual. The lights inside were turned up, and a crowd was chattering. Marty was doing a land-office business.

Pat greeted me, "Glad you're here. You know how to organize things."

Pat was right. I've had experience organizing things, but not a trial, and not a trial for God. Pat yelled. "Listen up. Mickey here's gonna help us get started."

People looked at me, and I looked around. No one was laughing. I wasn't sure where to start. Marty agreed to be the judge, but that was all we had.

"All right," I said. "We have a judge, and there'll be no jury. So, we only need someone to ask questions and witnesses to testify. I'm thinking maybe two or three for the prosecution and the same for the defense. Pat should be the lead-off witness for the prosecution since this was all his idea."

Finding witnesses to defend God should be no problem in a Catholic town, but finding people who want to testify against Him—not so easy. And since Pat started this ruckus, I told him to find another witness and left it with him. A week would give Pat time to find a witness or change his mind.

———— ⬤⬤⬤ ————

A week later, when I got home, I said to my wife, "Turn on Fox News. They interviewed Pat. He was sober and dead serious."

...This is Ron Reynolds for Fox News, coming to you live from the site of a most unusual event. Some men in a bar called the Boar's Head got into a heated argument about God and ended up deciding to put God on trial for malfeasance. They have organized a trial, and bar owner Marty Matthews is to serve as a judge. Unfortunately, there's no room for our camera and equipment inside, but we've interviewed people leaving the bar.

Pat Robinson, the man who started the affair, has some details...

Mr. Robinson, was it your idea to put God on trial?

It was. I have questions. The world's going to pot, and not the marijuana kind. If God is so great, why all the mess?

What do you think might be the outcome?

I've no idea. We'll have to wait and see. I doubt if it will be "Lock him up."

Rose continued cutting lettuce for a salad. "I thought you and your buddies would have forgotten about it by now. Turn that nonsense off. No wonder nobody watches the news anymore."

I left for the pub right after breakfast the next Sunday. Half the town was there. The reporter was talking into the camera:

...Ambulances have taken away a couple of people who fainted because of the crowd, but the people are orderly. There is no police presence or any other sort of crowd control...

Ye gods! I thought. *This has turned into a circus.*

I had to go around to the back to get past the security. Marty was behind the bar, busy as a hamster. He ordered more supplies for the curious who came to see the place where God was on trial. And he arranged two tables, like an American court, for the prosecution and the defense. One of the chairs on the defense side looked more like a throne.

"Marty, what's with the fancy chair?"

"Out of respect, you know. All this makes me nervous. I'd like to get back to normal. I'll tell you one thing. If it turns out bad, I'll personally package Pat and send him someplace where he doesn't even speak the language. See if he can talk his way out of that."

The onlookers were whispering like they were in a mortuary or at the bedside of a sick person.

Marty picked up a gavel, moved just to the left of the beer taps, and banged on the bar. "Okay, folks, settle down. Show a little respect! We'll begin with a reading of the charges and follow with testimony from the side bringing the charges. Then the defense will have a chance to—to defend. Then I'll give you my decision." Marty came up with a Bible, which he placed on the bar.

Pat walked to the bar and put his hand on the Bible. "I swear to tell the truth, the whole truth, and nothing but the truth, so help me."

"You mean, 'So help me God,' don't you?"

"No. I mean I'm going to tell the truth."

Marty shrugged and said, "Okay. So, who's gonna question Pat?"

A middle-aged man in an expensive suit came out of the crowd. "Your honor, I'm Justin Farrington of the law firm of Brown, Baker, Lithgow, and Farrington. When we heard about your situation in Providence, I called Mr. Patterson to see if we could assist. Since this is an informal court, I see no reason to produce my credentials, but I can if necessary."

Pat looked a little smug, like he had pulled off a coup. A murmur came from the spectators, and Marty said, "Okay. Get on with it."

Farrington began, "Mr. Robinson, please state your name and give your city of residence."

"My name is Pat Robinson. I was born and grew up in this here village. Other than two years in the military and two years in college, this is my home and will be till I die."

"Mr. Robinson, you're charging God with malfeasance. Do you know what malfeasance means?"

"Yes. It means holding an office and not carrying out the duties properly."

"You say you have evidence God is not carrying out His duties. What do you believe those duties to be?"

"The Church teaches us God has all power, knows everything, past, present, and future, and He's just and good."

"So, you don't disagree with what the church teaches? You're only alleging God is not doing His job, correct?"

"Correct."

Farrington said, "Then would you explain your allegations?"

Pat took a notebook from his jacket, opened it, and looked at his notes.

"First, what about Kerry's son over in Providence? When my son did some wheelies down by the off-ramp, the patrolmen brought him to my front door, said I should talk to him, got in their patrol car, and drove away. When Kerry's son was stopped, not by one but two patrolmen, for what they said was a broken taillight, they got him out of his car, gave him a sobriety test, took him to the station, and fingerprinted him. His dad had to go get him out, and they had to pay towing and storage to get his car out of the impound. Black lives matter, you know. Where's the justice?"

Farrington said, "Are you blaming all injustices on God? Do you think God should run everyone's life?"

Pat said, "He should stop injustice, yes. Unfortunately, it appears more like He's hiding in a corner."

Some of the crowd looked at each other and nodded as if Pat were speaking for them, too.

"Is there more evidence you want to give?"

Pat continued. "Well, we all know Bobby McEwan, James and Jenny's only child. He was six and doing good in first grade. He got sick, and died a few days later."

Some of McEwan's neighbors nodded and whispered to each other.

"Quiet, please," Marty said. "We're not taking sides. We're taking testimony."

Pat went on, "Bobby will never grow up, marry, have a family, or grow old with his grandchildren around him. So, why didn't God protect him? What's the use of a child living only six years?"

Farrington said, "We'll all die. So, why should it matter when we go, young or old?"

"When we get old, we've had a turn at-bat. We've had a life. But why is a kid born if he's only going to live six years? Taking a six-year-old is not right."

Farrington said, "So you think we should never even get sick?"

"Not necessarily, but dying so young is wrong. God has the power to protect Bobby, and He didn't."

Farrington led Pat on. "You have one more case where you charge God with malfeasance. Please explain."

"What are we reading about the Kurds? Our country took them on board. Now we're making them walk the plank. Why has God allowed us to betray them and potentially wipe them out? Aren't they the good guys? Yet, on newscasts, we see men in city streets firing automatic weapons. What must their wives and children be going through? What did they do to deserve getting caught in the crossfire? I call it malfeasance."

"Is this your personal experience?"

"No. But, now that you mention it, how does it happen that I have an easy life while people in *other* parts of the world get abused and shot at? I bet they're as good as I am. They have families, just like me."

Farrington asked, "Do you have anything more to add?"

"One last thing," said Pat. "I have petitions here sent to me by post and over the internet in the last weeks. Thousands of people are asking the same questions. They think God could do a better job policing the world." He handed a stack of papers to Farrington, who passed them on to Marty, who laid them aside.

Farrington said, "Thank you, Mr. Robinson." Then he turned to the other table and said, "Your witness."

As Barney McGill, a local lawyer, rose from his chair at the defense table, a strong jolt shook the building. Some ducked under tables. Others near the door ran outside. Most looked frightened, not knowing what to do. We waited. A second shock never came, and everybody took a deep breath.

"No harm done," said Marty. "There might be an aftershock, but it won't be as strong as this one. This is a good place to stop. We'll take up here next Sunday. Who wants a beer?"

T he following week, by the time I got there, everything seemed in place and ready to go. Marty said, "Pat's still under oath. Let's get on with the defense."

Barney McGill rose and approached Pat. "Mr. Robinson," he said, "Do you admit to being human?"

Pat smiled. "I'd have to say I do."

"Then," said McGill, "your knowledge is limited."

"It is."

"So, no matter what the big picture is, you are not capable of comprehending the entire operation of the world. Is that correct?"

"True."

"Is it possible God is acting properly, and you simply do not understand what God is doing?"

"Possibly, but I'm not blind. I can see what's going on here and around the world. People are starving, taken into slavery, treated like cattle."

McGill said, "But do you admit there could be a higher purpose you are not aware of?"

"My father told me, 'If you want to feed your family, don't rob a bank; get a job. *How* you do something is just as important as what you aim to do.' God should look at His methods. How could anyone say the death of masses of people contributes to a greater good?"

The building shook and a loud crack sounded. People looked at each other, but no one panicked. Marty said, "Okay, folks. We've had this before. Calm down, and we'll continue."

A bit rattled, McGill went on, "Do you believe in free will, where a person is free to make bad choices as well as good ones?"

"I do, but I don't think Bobby McEwan made a bad choice at age 6. I don't think Kerry's son chose to be black. I don't think millions of Armenians, blacks, and Jews who were exterminated made bad choices."

Pat sat down, and Farrington said. "Call Jason Jones."

Jason came forward and took the oath correctly, "so help me, God," and stood to Marty's left.

"Mr. Jones," said Farrington, "are you in agreement with the charge of malfeasance? Is it your testimony that God is not doing a good job managing the world?"

Jason said, "It is. It seems like God treats the world like a child playing with toy soldiers. He puts us in situations where someone always gets hurt, and He shows no signs He cares for us. Why doesn't He do something—anything? If we don't get an explanation, what are we to think? Does He want us ignorant? Why doesn't He communicate with us?"

Farrington said, "Thank you, Mr. Jones." Then he turned to Barney McGill and said, "Your witness."

The room began to buzz, but Marty shut them down. "Order! Quiet!"

McGill said, "Mr. Jones, we all know you. You're in mass as much as any man among us. Are you a man of faith?"

"I am."

"Then do you believe in life after death?"

"The way I see it, there has to be. Good people should get a reward, and bad people should be punished for the wrongs they do. So, yes. I believe in life after death."

McGill said, "Then why are you here, testifying that God is guilty of malfeasance when you believe in the end, justice will be done?"

"The world suffers a lot of pain and evil while we wait in hope life will someday be fair and just. I hope it's true, but what if we're wrong?" The quiet chatter suggested Jason had voiced concerns held by several of those listening.

Marty spoke up, "I think we've heard enough for today. We'll finish the defense next week. So, drink up and enjoy. Happy Sabbath."

When I got home, I turned on the TV news. The reporter was saying:

...Ron, bring us up to date on the trial you're covering. What's going on?

Today, an earthquake shook the building, and people almost panicked. It only lasted seconds, but some people wondered if it might be a sign. However, we live near a fault. A quake now and then, we take in stride.

So, when will we get the next installment of our drama?

They expect to conclude testimonies next Sunday...

Rose surprised me when Sunday came and she said, "We'd better go early, or we might not get inside. Father Francis will understand."

Like before, I parked about a block away, and we walked down the alley to the back entrance. Marty had doubled the security.

Only a small rectangle of the floor was visible in front of the bar. People whispering produced a steady hum. Marty was in high spirits, greeting people and serving from behind the bar. When the time came, he gaveled the room to order.

"All right," he said, "let's get started. Today it's time for the defense."

Emerging from the crowd came Father Francis wearing his vestments with a biretta covering his bald spot. When he gave Rose the eye, she looked like a kid caught taking money from the collection box. He walked past her to Marty's left and raised his hand. "I swear to tell the God's awful truth and nothing but."

Marty said, "Father, aren't you forgetting?"

"I'm forgetting nothing."

"Sorry, Father. I thought—"

"We're not here to listen to what you think. Get on with it."

"What do you have in mind, Father?"

"I don't need McGill to question me. I know the questions."

Marty said, "Then please, Father, proceed."

Father Francis began, "We all know and love Pat Robinson. He has not always attended mass, but he always pitches in when we try to raise money for the church. Pat's troubled because things in the world seem chaotic—and rightfully so. Nobody's disputing that. The question is: what responsibility does God have for the chaos? And the answer, of course, is none. God is a God of order, not chaos. We see it plainly with the movement of the stars and changing of the seasons. The entire universe is like a giant computer with its parts moving in perfect order."

Pat, emboldened by his recent time in the spotlight, nudged Farrington, who said, "Begging your pardon, Father, but we're not talking about the universe. We're talking about the earth and the mess the world's in."

Father Francis, unaccustomed to being challenged and slightly flustered, said, "Right. Well, what appears like chaos on earth is chaos from a human perspective. The divine perspective is different."

Farrington again, "How do we know that, Father?"

"We know it by faith," Father Francis said. "There's no other way."

Farrington had a look of wonder on his face. "So, Father, there is no other way? It's faith or nothing?"

Father Francis said, "That's about the sum of it. You believe, or you don't."

"There's no real evidence? Just faith?"

"Faith. That's the final answer."

"I rest my case," said Farrington.

———————————∞————————————

All eyes turned to Marty. He gave a deep sigh, paused, and said, "We've heard the testimony. We can't deny the facts. But we also don't know what the end of the story will be. Will there be justice later? Is there 'pie in the sky by and by?' Pat and Jason made good points. The world is full of injustice and chaos. Father Francis' answer takes the long view held by many people. God has been silent. He neither defends Himself nor offers explanations. We can't deny the reality of the world around us, but there's always the unknown, an element of mystery. And we have no answers, except, like Father Francis says, faith. Lacking more evidence, I say we have a mistrial on our hands."

Pat jumped out of his chair. "I object! Just because God doesn't come to His own defense doesn't let Him off the hook. The world needs serious fixing! Saying God is going to fix it someday is not enough!"

The people in the room got excited and began to argue.

To my surprise, Pat's face turned from anger to stone. Jaws clenched, he walked over to Marty. "Two bottles of whiskey," he said and dropped a wad of cash on the bar. Marty hesitated then hoisted them from under the bar. Pat said, "I'm going fishing." He marched out of the room, a bottle in each hand. As he passed, he spoke to his wife. "Don't worry. I'll be back when I get back."

Fox News reporters stopped Pat on his way out, but as he stalked past, Pat said, "I've nothing to say to you. We can't even acknowledge the state our world is in or admit God's doing nothing about it."

He pulled out of the parking lot and drove the short distance to the dock, where he secured the bottles on his skiff and headed out to sea. His boat disappeared over the horizon while we watched in silence.

O n Monday, Pat's wife called me and said his boat had been sighted in the bay, and the only thing on the boat was an almost empty bottle of whiskey.

We formed an organized search party so no part of the nearby sea would go unsearched. The weather was ideal, the sea was calm, but we found no debris or any sign of Pat's body. Police helicopters swept the area for hours. Finally, after searching and crisscrossing the area all day, near sunset, we came in for the night. Had we seen the last of Pat? His well-known propensity to drink too much, his state of mind, and his feelings about the trial didn't give us much hope.

Wednesday evening, as we discussed a plan for Pat's service, sorrow was dripping like an IV in a hospital room.

"He was a good man despite his faults."

"He was a good father to his children."

"He was always a man with strong convictions."

"He shouldn't have got so upset. For what?"

"And I remember, even when he disagreed, he stated his opinions like a gentleman. We'll miss him."

"Now, Molly must manage on her own. We'll have to look after her."

Even Father Francis pointed out that, although Pat had more doubt than faith, and more questions than answers, he had more courage than most of us, and after all, he said, "He was religious."

Rose was eager for a report when I arrived home. "What did you boys decide?" she asked.

"When we were about to finalize the details, we were interrupted, and a fight almost broke out."

"A fight! Again? You must be kidding. How can a fight break out during preparations for a wake?"

"We were nursing our drinks, recalling stories about Pat. We agreed to wait a respectable time, so Marty put the money we collected in his safe. About 9:00, the door swung open, and in came an elderly man, followed by none other than Pat Robinson. His clothes were a little soiled, but he was carrying his purple life jacket we all recognized. We jumped up and closed in on him, and said, 'Pat! Man! We thought you were dead! Where have you been? What happened?'

Pat introduced us to his new friend and rescuer Fred, and his wife. They hauled Pat off the beach, put him to bed, and took care of him. Well, you know how upset he was after the trial. As usual, he tried to drown it in drink. When he was turning to come in, he fell overboard. His lifejacket kept him afloat, but he was too drunk to get back in the boat. He said, the harder he tried, the sleepier he got. Before he knew it, the boat had drifted away, and there he was, floating like a cork.'

"Marty put a beer in Pat's hand and encouraged Pat to continue. Pat said the tide took him north, and eventually, he washed up on the shore by Grover's Cove. He was out of his head for a day or two, but they took care of him like a baby and wouldn't let him do a thing.'

"'We asked him why he didn't let us know.

"Pat said they have no telephone, and they're not even on the highway. He told us he could have got back a little sooner, then he flashed that broad grin of his, and said, knowing us, he'd give us an extra day. He thought by now we'd have him canonized and he could pop in and surprise us.

"All the men rose, ready to pummel him.

"Marty was gasping for breath when he said, 'You no good son of your father! Do you have any idea what you put us through? You're not a saint, you—you rat!'"

Hearing my account, Rose smiled sweetly and said, "Knowing the boys, I'm sure you forgave Pat."

And in time, we did forgive Pat. I can't speak for God.

This Old House

Living in a house for 45 years, one collects memories galore. One week was filled with galore.

Tuesday morning, the ice cream in our fridge was getting soft. I went into panic mode and called a well-advertised repair service.

"We can't get to you for two days," they said.

I made an appointment for Thursday, but I kept looking for someone who could come sooner. Several calls later, I found a repairman who could come on Wednesday.

Meanwhile, during a telephone call to my brother several states away, I mentioned our problem. He said, "When did you last vacuum under your refrigerator? It's not complicated, and it might save you a service charge." It was worth a try.

To clean under the fridge, it was necessary to remove a series of hexagonal screws that held the back cover on. After a brief search, I found the right screwdriver and removed the back, revealing a whole warren of dust bunnies.

The needle-nosed vacuum attachment sucked the fuzz from under, over, and around every visible surface. My wife and I retired that night, hoping that the freezer would be working normally in the morning, but on Wednesday morning the ice cream was still soft.

A few hours later, a repairman pushed our fridge away from the wall, pleased that the back was already off. He knelt to get a better look. I stood behind him, shining a flashlight over his head into the dark cavity. The farther he bent over, the lower his belt crept, until finally another dark cavity came into view. His butt crack smiled up at me like a . . . well, like a butt crack. I said nothing.

His examination complete, he rose, hiked up his pants, and announced: "Either the heater, or the fan, or the computer chip has malfunctioned. I don't work on any of those. You'll have to call someone else." He left without charging for the call.

<hr />

The next repairman, slated to arrive between 3:00 and 5:00, showed up about 6:30, without apology, and demanded payment. After pocketing my check, he glanced at the freezer and announced that the frost build-up showed him which part had failed.

"We don't have that part in stock," he said. "I'll have to order one. I can install it Saturday." He congratulated us on our nine-year-old refrigerator. "You're lucky yours has lasted so long. Most fridges need new parts after only five years."

When I saw his estimate, I said, "Maybe it would be cheaper to buy a new one."

"No," he insisted. "Your design is a style that's no longer being manufactured. It's the best ever made." He added, "If you defrost the freezer yourself, that might save some labor costs when we install the new part."

With little time to spare, our son hurried over from across town and, in short order, drove away with the melting contents of our freezer in the trunk of his Mercury.

The repairman's defrosting instructions were simple: "To defrost the fridge, unplug it. Catch the water as the ice melts." What he failed to mention was that water would drain from several different spots, at random intervals, hour after hour, all through the night. Every time we spotted a puddle, we caught it with a towel so as not to damage our floors. By morning, every towel in the house was wet.

A s I was gathering wet towels to put in the dryer, my wife came in from the laundry room and announced, "Our dryer's broken."

"What? Do we have a service contract for it?"

"No," she said. "We don't."

Hoping to save money, I called the repair service. "Can the repairman due back on Saturday replace the heating element in the dryer at the same time?"

The clerk said that for an additional charge, he could look at it—not fix it, just look at it.

Our son who had saved the ice cream advised that replacing the heating element in a dryer is easy. So, using my online list of businesses, I began calling.

Again and again, I heard the words: "The parts would have to be ordered." Surely, I thought, in a city of a half million people, parts should be available locally. At last, a clerk asked, "Is there any heat at all?"

"The unit gets warm, but not hot enough to dry clothes."

He said, "The heating element in a dryer is like a light bulb. It's either on or off. There's no halfway. If there is a little heat, then the problem is not the heating element. Have you cleaned the lint trap lately?"

Was he kidding? We religiously cleaned our lint trap after every load. Still, I disconnected the vent pipe and looked in.

It didn't look dirty from my end. My wife removed the lint trap from the dryer door and poked around. She said, "I feel something soft." She kept on poking while I retreated into the kitchen and closed the door behind me.

A few minutes later, she dashed in from the laundry room and slammed the door, looking like she had just walked through a giant spider web.

"What happened?" I said.

Out of breath, she stammered, " ... I turned the dial ... pushed the start button ... and heard a small rattling sound ... Suddenly lint and dust ... shot out of the dryer ... The walls are covered ... it's hanging from the ceiling."

I helped her un-decorate herself.

To fix the dryer meant replacing the tube that ran from the back of the dryer through the garage wall into a flower bed in the front yard. To do so, one must open the garage in the front of the house.

Opening the garage door proved to be almost impossible. One of the giant coiled springs that held the door open lay broken on the garage floor. That necessitated a trip to Home Depot, where the clerk directed me to aisle 9 for the vent, and aisle 21 for the spring. I picked up a tube for the dryer, then went in search of a spring.

I learned that there was no "one size fits all" for springs. Did I need the 28", the 30", or the 32"? I took a chance and bought a 30". Arriving home and placing it beside the broken spring, I saw another trip to Home Depot in my immediate future.

Installing the 28" spring required two people, one to hold the garage door open to a height of about eight feet, the other to attach the spring. Our son came to our aid for a third time. I held the door up; he attached it, and it worked perfectly. He also attached the new vent tube to the dryer in only a few minutes. We started and stopped the dryer a few times till the noise of tumbling debris died out. It worked fine.

***

By Saturday afternoon, the refrigerator repairman arrived to install the part and collect a check for the original estimate—all without acknowledging our all-night vigil. Finally, after four days, our refrigerator was restocked, the towels were dry, and we celebrated by opening and closing the garage door several times—just for fun.

The Body Shoppe

M y wife died on our 47th anniversary. Two years later, at 70, I still got the urges common to all males past puberty. But I would never have guessed technology could solve my problem.

In the clubhouse locker room, my friend Hayden smiled and said, "You heard about Jim?"

"Tell me," I said. We all knew Hayden enjoyed locker room gossip.

"Jim went to a new store on the mall and exchanged bodies with a young man! For two days, he packed in everything he could think of."

"How did he do that?"

"He went to a store that has an app that lets two people trade bodies. Think about it. We could be young again—for a price," he said, grinning.

"That sounds amazing. How does it work?"

"They have a stable of healthy young people willing to exchange bodies with an older person for a day or two. The kids make a bundle for a couple of days of inconvenience. You trade bodies but keep your personalities. Then when your time's up, you both revert to your normal selves."

The idea was intriguing. A romp in a younger body might be worth considering. I thought it over for several days. Sex without a relationship is normal, a biological act animals do routinely. And if both parties accept the idea of casual sex, no one gets hurt. Admittedly, shelling out a large amount of money for a one-night stand doesn't make all that much sense. But recalling the early days of my marriage, the intensity of sex with a much younger body was a strong pull. I had the money and the desire, so I decided to go for it.

I went to the mall and found the store. A banner over the entrance proclaimed: Live your Fantasy! and a sign over the door read: The Body Shoppe. The owner, a man of about 40, built like he didn't need the service he was peddling, greeted me.

"Come in!" he almost shouted.

Life-sized posters of young, attractive couples covered the walls, and at the back were two upright transparent cylinders, about 8 feet tall.

"This is where the magic takes place," he said. "And it's painless. Lasts for as long as you want, then you're back to your normal self. Fully insured and approved by the FDA."

"Sit here and make yourself comfortable. I'll pull up the file to show you our employees," he said.

I flipped through holograms of young men, all healthy, clean looking. Finally, I stopped on one about my size, with dark hair like I once had, a friendly face, and a baritone voice. "Is the charge the same for all of them?"

"Yes, a flat rate. You interested in Donovan?" he said, indicating the man showing on my monitor.

"I am."

"The shortest time you can buy is 24 hours. The price for a day goes down by 50% past the first day. The set-up is the big cost."

Despite the cost, which amounted to an entire month of my retirement income, I signed a waiver of responsibility and paid for 24 hours.

On Saturday morning, I arrived at 8:00 A.M. for my appointment. The clerk told me to "dress young," so I wore jeans and a sports shirt. Donovan showed up; we smiled at each other and shook hands.

"I've done this a few times," Donovan said. "Don't do anything I wouldn't do." He laughed.

Each of us got into one of the cylinders. The clerk locked the chambers and moved to a console where he pushed some buttons. It didn't take long, and I only felt a slight vibration, but I stepped out of the cylinder and my hands were those of a young man. Donovan got out of the other cylinder, but slowly. Yes, he had my body.

A s I drove away, I reviewed my plans. I had already discarded the idea of searching for someone at a movie theater. A grocery store aisle might work, but I settled on the golf course at my club.

I waited on a bench near the first hole like a spider hoping for a fly. Four women came out of the clubhouse and moved to the first tee. Each teed her ball and drove down the fairway. They were laughing as they walked away. A couple of men followed them. Then, my luck changed.

A young woman about Donovan's age got out of her car, unloaded her cart and clubs, and came past the bench where I sat. She was alone. Her embossed leather golf bag looked expensive.

She was a picture. I admired her tall, willowy stance as she teed up her ball, drew back her driver, and swung with force. She missed!

"May I help you?" I asked. "Are you a beginner?"

"That was an easy guess," she said with a smile. Her eyes got brighter. Donovan's body was doing its job.

"I can help, if you'll permit me."

"Would you mind? You can see I'm pretty much a beginner."

I moved to where she stood, and her perfume, though not strong, was like smoke from a magic lantern.

"This might be a bit forward, but I'll have to put my arms around you to show you how to fix your swing."

"Of course," she said, "if you're not allergic." She let out a small laugh.

My arms reached around her, and I put my hands on hers, gripping the club. Her hands were soft.

"Remember, you're not aiming for the ball, but you're swinging your club on a path that goes through the ball as if the ball was a hologram. The smoother your swing, the farther it goes."

She took four practice swings before placing the ball on the tee. Then, she swung hard. The ball soared down the fairway quite far for a woman.

"Lucky shot!" She was elated.

"With that kind of luck, you could win a tournament."

She smiled and said, "That's only one shot."

I teed up and drove my ball about the same distance she had gone. There were no players behind us, so we strolled down the fairway. It turned out she had not played for a long time and felt the need to get out more, and she was alone. "The clubs," she said, "belonged to my late husband."

I told her I, too, was a widower, and that I understood her feeling of loss and the difficulty of adjusting. For a second, I thought she was going to tear up, but she took a deep breath, pursed her lips, and took her second shot.

We continued to play and chat as we walked. By the time we reached the ninth hole, the weather had warmed up, and I had learned her husband had died only a short while ago. I said, "Since this is a new activity for you, perhaps you shouldn't overdo it your first time out."

"I am tired," she said, and we sat on the grass in the shade of a giant elm.

"It's past noon. How about we get a bite? There are some good restaurants in this part of town."

"That's thoughtful of you, but I couldn't impose."

"We could get better acquainted," I said.

"I planned a light snack at home. How about sharing my lunch?"

Was she kidding? I said, "I'd love to."

I followed her car to an affluent part of town near the golf course.

She cut the crusts off her chicken salad sandwiches and placed a pickle spear beside them. A fruit bowl finished the menu. We sat on high stools around a granite-topped kitchen island.

"What would you like to drink? I have a cold beer if you like," she asked.

"Whatever you're having is fine."

"Iced tea coming up."

After the meal, we sat in silence till she moved her hand to cover mine and looked at me.

I felt aroused, but I needed to be sure.

"Should I go?" I asked, hoping she would say no.

"Please stay," she said, an open invitation. My venture was about to pay off, and my hormones were raging. Then the worst happened. My brain kicked in, and I made the mistake of thinking.

She was a vulnerable widow, and I was a fake. She needed care and understanding, friendship, before moving to the stage I was contemplating.

I told my conscience to give me a break, but it wouldn't shut up. *You'll be gone in a few hours. She needs a relationship, not a roll in the hay. Tomorrow, when you're gone, what's she left with?*

I could feel my heart crumbling like a day-old cookie. I faced an ogre of guilt. It was hard, but I forced myself to say, "I'm sorry. I must go. It'll be better for you if I just disappear."

She almost pleaded, "Can't you stay? For a little while?"

I had to escape before I weakened. I opened the door, jacket in hand, and turned to see a tear on her cheek. I bolted for my car. My 24 hours couldn't be over soon enough. I desperately wanted to return to being a lonely old man unwilling to injure someone. I still had standards, and I was better off being myself in the real world and not playacting.

S unday morning, after I got my own body back, I felt like a sad, noble failure. I had spent a lot of money and all I got for it was a small shred of self-respect.

I was suffocating in the house, so I headed for the golf course, but not to the clubhouse where my friends would expect a full report. Instead, I sat on the bench at the first tee, trying some slow breathing to get back to the real world. Finally, groups filtered out of the clubhouse and began their rounds.

After about 45 minutes, a lone woman more in my age range drove up, unloaded her clubs, and headed for the first hole. She was stately and exuded quality, a classy lady.

As she strolled past me, I noticed her embossed leather golf bag. I waited while she teed up. Her technique wasn't bad, but she sliced the ball to the far right. Shaking my head in amusement, I thought, *Some neighbors are probably picking her golf ball out of their pool this very moment.*

I smiled as I walked over to her and said, "May I help you with your swing?"

Cardiac Floor Plan

My heart it has four chambers,
Four chambers has my heart,
And had it not four chambers,
It would not be my heart.

Two rooms are in the upstairs,
Two rooms are down below,
The atria let the blood in,
The ventricles let it go.

Say thrice: the upper atria,
Say ventricles three times, too.
There is no space for closets,
No attic, basement, or loo.

My *other* heart has many,
Too many rooms to count.
They come and go, the plan's in flux,
There is no set amount.

M y *other* heart once had a room called *Thievery*, displaying chalk, a silver dollar, and a cheat sheet.

First, I stole a stub of chalk from my fifth-grade classroom. My desk was near the chalkboard, and I wanted the chalk. For what? I had no board at home and no sidewalk to play a game on. But the chalk drew me to it. So, I put it in my pocket and walked home, head held high, like a law-abiding citizen. I do not remember what happened to the chalk; nor does it matter, but the act left a scar.

Second, I only had money for specific purposes, like 10 cents for a trip to the movies or to buy a loaf of bread. I never had "walking around" money. So, when rummaging through my Mother's chest of drawers at age 10 or 11, I came across a silver dollar. Without considering the consequences, I took it and spent it.

When Mother missed it, she asked me if I knew anything about it. No, I lied. Then, she told me it was a keepsake from my older brother, her fourth son, who was killed in Germany in WWII and buried in a Belgian cemetery among white crosses stretching out of sight.

The longer I thought about it, the worse I felt. I cried, not on the outside but inside, ashamed I had thoughtlessly stolen and wasted something precious to the one person who meant the world to me. I broke down and confessed—and she dismissed it. Having a silver dollar in your hand is never the same as holding your son in your arms.

I concluded my career as a thief by stealing knowledge—information. I mined it out of an eighth-grade English textbook to cheat on a test. Unaware my teacher, Mrs. Wolfe, with her silver hair, powdered face, and rimless glasses, had left her desk and was moving around the room, I moved my leg to see the cheat sheet beneath it. But when I looked down for an answer, instead, I saw a black leather shoe and, above it, a thick ankle. As my eyes slowly rose, my body felt like it was on fire.

Mrs. Wolfe crushed me with a look I still remember 75 years later—a lingering look of profound disappointment. Her gaze deep into my soul was greater punishment than being placed on the rack. The weight of her silence was suffocating me. Repentance washed over me, and I vowed never to cheat again. And I never did. Well, maybe once, but onto the next room.

∽∽

While I successfully closed the *Thievery* room in my heart, for several years, I struggled with a room marked *Hate*. It only took one sentence for hate to enter and make itself at home.

This middle-aged man and I worked together at a lumber mill. I was a self-satisfied Christian, so right that I squeaked at every turn, while he, the newcomer, was uneducated, common. After we had worked together for a short while, out of the blue, he blurted out, "Don't beg me to come to church. I'll come if I want to." Inviting him to attend church had not crossed my mind although it should have. I should have said, "You are precious to God. Whether you come to church or not, God loves you."

Instead, I thought, *Do you think you're special? Who asked you to come to church? I didn't. What a presumption!* Years later the mere thought of the man brought my resentment to the surface. I feared I might die with that monster still nestled in my heart.

Eventually, I grew ashamed because I came to see I was like a Pharisee who admired his own righteousness and scorned outsiders. Self-righteousness is no one's servant, but a Master Alchemist whose poison taints every room in the heart.

So, I prayed many times, asking God to loosen this bond. Then one day, my shame dissolved. The torment disappeared, and I closed that room.

∽∽

Another small, overcrowded room I keep open for *Regret*. It is small because I don't want to dwell on my regrets. It is crowded because I have a goodly number of words and actions that stock the room. From my brother's 1937 college yearbook, I learned: "It is better to be silent and be thought dumb than to speak and remove all doubt."

<hr>

From an early age, my heart has had a *Music* room that brightens every part of my heart. To describe how important music has been in my life would be like explaining how blood has been important. There is no way to measure it.

I taught myself to play by pounding on the piano day after day until something sounded good to my ear. One of the earliest memories of my mother is of her standing over me in the living room where I had been playing incessantly. With eyes bugging out and hands in the air, she said, "Wayland, if you don't stop, I'm going to pull my hair out." My dad's method was equally direct but simpler: He rattled his newspaper and said, "Let it rest." It rested instantly, end of story.

Nonetheless, the pathway of music led through the Grand Ole Opry; the New York Metropolitan Opera at the cinema every Saturday; to countless churches, accompanying hymn singing, leading youth and adult choirs, and composing a few pieces, including a short opera. For a couple of decades, I played the piano at the Fresno Rescue Mission. Today I play oldies in senior-assisted living places across Fresno and Clovis while residents eat lunch or dinner. And like many musicians, I play in my brain while falling asleep.

<hr>

Only after I had reached middle age did a door to a vast roomful of Questions gradually begin to open. Up till then, I had very little experience in independent thinking. I received religious dogma like a baby bird sitting in a nest with its beak open, waiting for its mother to feed it. Change finally got a toehold after I adopted as one of my mottos: *Always question assumptions.*

I had to dig deep for courage to ask some unanswerable questions. For example: *What is the purpose of life? Is there a*

God? Is there an afterlife? Is the Bible necessary for religion? Is organized religion legitimate? And more.

One important aspect of this room was learning to be honest with myself about who I am, which is still a struggle. During that metamorphosis, I gradually approached the mirror. Getting a glimpse of my true self helped me to accept others as they are because, while I continue to revise my own life and share with anyone who will listen, I am not into revising others' lives. I have no "secrets" to pass on.

Yet another room, once open, is now only slightly ajar, an Art room full of paintings and drawings. I took classes and experimented with #2 pencils and watercolors. My pieces include a self-portrait, and a portrait of Vestee Jackson, a student I taught to read at the Fresno Rescue Mission. Over time, I learned about three-dimensional drawing, the hues and intensity of colors, the color wheel, vanishing points, and facial and body proportions. My favorite pencil drawing is a hallway in Fresno State's art department, showing shades ranging from off-white to charcoal black. A view of El Capitan, in Yosemite Valley, is my favorite ink drawing. When my interest in painting and drawing waned, I gave my paraphernalia to my grandson, a budding artist in his own right. Many of my pieces are posted on my website:

https://waylandjackson.com/

It sounds simple, perhaps even simple-minded, but I keep hoping the largest room in my heart is Love—accepting my uniqueness and respecting the uniqueness of others. Loving eliminates many other rooms. In alphabetical order, rooms like Anger, Apathy, Distrust, Envy, Hate, Ignor-Ance, Ill-Will, Jealousy, Snobbery, and Stereotyping, among others.

I learned: Never love something that can't love you back. Don't love money, your job, your boat or car, your house or office, your clothes, or your reputation. Love your wife, husband, partner, parents, children, friends, neighbors, and—your enemies. If the love is returned, that's a plus. If it isn't, you're still ahead because you can still respect yourself.

Waiting

He had spent a lot of his life waiting. He waited for his first-grade classroom door to open, proud to enter and take his seat, instantly in love with Miss Milam and her blond hair, intoxicated by the fragrance of her talcum powder.

He waited four months for a report card in seventh grade, and even though it had a humiliating "D," the lowest grade he had ever received, he took it home dutifully. At least he had passed.

He had waited for the "nickel bus" to take him to school each day, and while waiting, had memorized "How do I love thee? Let me count the ways."

In lines in a gymnasium where the professors of the small college sat behind tables enrolling students for the opening term of the year—he waited. He waited in line for the dormitory dining hall to open, but not because the food was gourmet. On spaghetti night, Bill, who went on to become an astronaut, dished out spaghetti to those inching through the line. "Get your live fish bait right here!" *Presentation* was not big in the men's food service.

Four times he had waited in cap and gown to hear his name called, to march across a stage, to receive four pieces of paper which he still had somewhere.

He had waited in the anteroom till the usher said, "It's time." He took his place, and the wedding march began. In she came, floating down the aisle like an angel. She had been his savior in ways he had never imagined, absolutely worth waiting for.

He waited five hours, beginning at 2:30 A.M., watching Pacific waves dashing on rocks beneath a huge picture window till the birth pangs were over, and he had another love in his life.

When his mother died, he had waited in the viewing room. Friends and acquaintances came to pay their respects. He wondered where everyone was. Then it occurred to him that she had outlived most of her friends and acquaintances. Her heart was large enough to embrace the world, but she was not a public person. No one was going to come by representing some club or church. The family only, plus a few people he didn't know, all waited together.

Waiting with colleagues, marching in heavy rain, we struck for smaller classes. Others struck for more money. We didn't get smaller classes or more money. But we had stood up to power. We possessed a dignity we had never felt before.

I'm still waiting, he thought, in Room 103. I don't think we check out by room number. Leonard was in 104 but younger than me. One day he was there, the next he was gone, and now Franklin's in his room, waiting along with the rest of us.

Aggie loved to play Bingo, and she could keep three cards going at the same time since each number was called several times. She was lucky and the prizes were not bad—a candy bar, a small stuffed toy, or a knitted hand warmer someone had donated. They rolled the gurney past my door last night, and even with the sheet pulled over her face, I knew who it was.

So, what's next? he asked himself. The leap, that's what. The leap to the head of the line, the leap into . . . into what? He wondered where the idea had come from that there is something beyond death.

He thought of one of his Hmong students who had gone home ill one day. The next day Lao Moua had jumped to the head of the line. Alone, he had an epileptic seizure, fell off his bed, struck his head on the metal frame, and bled to death.

---

*T*he one indisputable fact is that we go. We might wait 100 years, or far less, but ultimately, we go, in war, by accident, on purpose, in the quiet of our home, or extracted from our room and hidden from view on a gurney.

He finally admitted to himself that notions of an afterlife—resurrection, heaven, purgatory—were all guesses that sprang from hope. The culture declares that saints reach heaven; sinners are assigned to hell; and wee sinners pass through purgatory where their souls do a turnaround. Perhaps none of that is real.

Over the years, he had gradually laid aside all ideas about life after death. Why speculate, he asked himself, when the answers never rise above the level of guesswork? Priests, ministers, gurus, and other specialists on the topic do not agree because they, too, are mere speculators.

Whatever happens after a person dies, he was content to leave in the hands of Other, his designation for divinity. But he took comfort in the fact that people who die live on—in our memories. People he had loved, people he had feared, people he might have only known casually, all lived inside his mind.

He still conjured up the phantoms of his mother and father. The smell of his father's aftershave. His mother, queen of the kitchen, waiting for the "third" table, the "women's" table, after the men, and then the children, had filled themselves with the holiday feast. He still heard the sweet voice of his blind Granny as she waited in her dark world, "Who's there? I know it's someone," when all along, she knew it was he.

He closed his eyes, wondering if this might be the last time he would close them. *If it is*, he thought, *then so be it.*

The Only Alien I Ever Met

L ooking at my title, your first question would be: *Are you insane?* Many of my fellow writers familiar with the fantasy and sci-fi genre talk freely about aliens, ETs, and creatures from other worlds. I, on the other hand, have never had the urge to speculate about aliens, their shapes and sizes, their intellect, or their desire to destroy or dominate the universe.

Therefore, when I encountered a critter, clearly not human and unlike any animal I had ever seen, even in National Geographic, I stared in wonder. Since I am not skilled in providing descriptions (a police officer would say I am an unreliable witness in identifying a suspect), I can only say the creature had what appeared to be two eyes. I could not even say it stood because I could not tell if it was touching the earth or hovering. Other than that, I will spare the reader the details of its appearance.

I figured it must have some sort of exotic powers. Where was it from? Was it intelligent? Might it kidnap me and perform weird experiments on me? If it gave me a test, would the test include calculus (not my strong point)? Could we communicate? Did it do Zoom meetings? Would it speak King James English and end its verbs in "-eth?"

Was it waiting for backup, or worse, doing a word search for the best recipe for preparing a human entrée? Fairly certain it didn't appreciate the significance of my gray hair; I was not tempted to flash my AARP membership card and ask for a senior discount on alien abduction. Yet, no longer the 98-pound weakling I once was as a kid, if it didn't let me go, I was ready to defend myself, still careful to make no movement that might provoke the thing.

When it did not move, I wondered if it might be as afraid of me as I was of it.

And how did it get here? I saw no spaceship or vehicle. Did it arrive in a transporter, like on Star Trek? Time and circumstances permitting, I rejected checking out the parking garage down the street, although I strongly doubted it came in a Ford or Chevy.

Expecting it to make the first move, I waited for what seemed like forever. Then without warning, I suddenly knew what it was thinking. Neither of us spoke, but we communicated. Telepathy? How weird, I thought.

It turned out its mission was not a hostile takeover of the planet. It was friendly. The visit was not planned, but an emergency. The alien was just passing by and needed a restroom—fast. I pointed it to a store, but it communicated that their restrooms were for customers only. I suggested I go with it and make a purchase while it used the facilities.

"You'd do that for me?" the alien asked.

"Why not?" I answered.

It worked out fine. The creature was relieved, and I invited it to come again. It promised to return as soon as it accumulated enough comp time. "Would it be okay if I brought a friend?" it asked.

Dinner on Sunday

A tall, gray-haired George Dandridge handed his topcoat to the cloakroom attendant, slipped the claim check in his pocket, and followed a waiter to his regular table at the Bartok's. After getting comfortable, he announced to his sons, "Of all our Sunday dinners over the past ten years, this should be the happiest. Ever since our first one after your mother died, you've both urged me countless times to update my will. You'll be glad to know I have an appointment with Morton to do just that this week."

Mark said, "As healthy as you are, you're not likely to need it any time soon. You go to the gym more than I do, for Chrissake. Still, it's better to take care of it. No need to remind you how Barry and I have fought over every bone in the yard since we were kids." He paused slightly. "And," he added, staring at his older brother, "we know who got most of the bones."

As soon as their drinks were served, they placed their orders. Dandridge liked his steaks rare; neither of his sons did. As soon as the waiter brought their salads and had gone away, Barry, the older brother, said, "I'm glad you're doing this, Dad."

"None of us has ever wanted for anything," Dandridge said, "thanks to my grandfather. Few people know his invention is the only part of the modern automobile that hasn't changed since cars were invented."

"True," said Barry smiling. "Those tire valves are still doing their job. We're lucky Great-grandfather had the good sense to invest his profits in Bell Telephone and Standard Oil."

"Thanks to Ma Bell and Rockefeller, you both stand to inherit great wealth. I've tried to set a good example for you. You know all the charities that have received large sums from our fortune. I've always believed others should benefit from what we've accumulated."

Staring unsmiling at his younger brother, Barry said, "Well at least one of us will carry on the family tradition. That's probably the best we can hope for."

Dandridge gritted his teeth, so his jaw muscles stood out. He folded his napkin, placed it by his plate, and pushed his chair back. "You fellows enjoy your dessert. I'm tired. I think I'll call it a night."

"You're taking your meds, aren't you, Dad?" asked Mark. "You're not Superman. We don't see you every day, so you're on your own to watch your blood pressure."

Dandridge lifted his brows slightly. "I feel good. I see no reason for you to worry," and he walked away.

Mark waited till his father was out of earshot. He looked Barry directly in the eye. "What do you think he's worth?" he asked.

"Do you mean 'What is *he* worth?' or 'How much *money* does he have?'"

"You know what I mean, jerk. He won't split it down the middle. You've always been his favorite," Mark said.

"That's because I don't borrow from everyone I meet. I'd be willing to bet, right now, you're holding off people you owe with a promise you're in line for a big payoff. You've always been stupid about money."

"I pay my bills."

"Be grateful for small blessings," Barry rolled his eyes. "You always take more risk than you can cover. Like when we went to school at Marshall, and Dad gave both of us $100 to give to the English teacher whose wife died. You gave him $50 and used the rest to pay off your bets on the New York Jets. You only pay your monthly bills because dad gives you an allowance. If you had your inheritance, you'd run through it like a Texas tornado."

"What about you, big brother? Still hanging onto the first dollar Dad ever gave you? Probably sleep with it under your pillow. I figured out why you've never married Grace after living together for four years."

"What do you mean?"

"I mean if you get your inheritance before you marry, it's all yours," said Mark. "If you marry after you inherit, it's community property. If she ever wanted to haul ass and quit your lousy company, it's half hers. That's what I mean."

"At least I have a relationship, which is more than you can say."

"If you want to call a live-in girlfriend who gives you freebies a relationship, be my guest."

"This discussion is pointless," said Barry. "I'm outta here."

The next morning Dandridge rose at 5:00 to workout in his state-of-the-art gym. He was in the kitchen with coffee brewing, before he spotted Mrs. Guerrero on the security camera walking up the driveway. At 8:00 he heard the lock in the front door turning and in came his housekeeper cook.

"Good morning, Mr. Dandridge. How are you feeling today?"

"Fine, thank you, Mrs. Guerrero. How about French toast for breakfast?"

"French toast, it is. I brought fresh strawberries. Shall I scramble you an egg?"

"That would be nice." Dandridge poured himself a cup of coffee and went through French doors to the table by the pool. He had finished the morning paper by the time she brought his food. The French toast was just the way he liked it, with a touch of cinnamon. "I'll be gone most of the morning, but I'll be back for lunch."

"Any special requests?"

"Surprise me. You're such a great cook. I'm lucky to have you."

After breakfast, Dandridge changed into a turtleneck sweater and slacks, left by his back door, walked past the pool, and entered the garage. He chose the MG because, by the time he came home, the weather would be warm enough for him to drive with the top down.

⌘

I nside a marbled building labeled Gregg and Dennison Law Firm, his lawyer greeted him. "George, how's it going? Come right in. Shirley, hold my calls."

"Good morning, Morton. I'm well, thanks. I'm here to update my will. My boys have been pushing me, so let's get it done."

"I agree with them. I've always been flabbergasted that a man of your wealth hasn't kept his will up to date. I'm so glad you came in today."

Dandridge sat at a mahogany conference table as Morton Gregg continued.

"I think we have a complete list of your holdings: stocks and bonds, property, your wife's art collection." He handed Dandridge several pages. "Look these over to see if you spot any omissions or discrepancies. You had a small army keeping an eye on your fortune before you retired. Now you seem relaxed, too relaxed. It's not like you to leave loose ends."

"I hope they'll all be tied up soon. I want your counsel. You know my boys. Barry's tightfisted. Mark's a loose cannon. I'll provide for them, but I also want to be sure my wealth does some good in the world. I wouldn't be happy with it just sitting in Barry's bank account, and I shudder to think how Mark might handle it."

"I don't know how you managed to raise two boys so different from each other."

"I don't know either. Once, when they were young, we took them on a picnic. Barry wanted to show how high he could climb in a tree. Mark grabbed his foot and dragged him to the ground. After a hard landing, Barry went crazy. We had to take them home. I was afraid one of them would hurt the other."

"I know they've never been fond of each other," Gregg said.

"We went to a school outing when the boys were at Marshall. Mark ran in a couple of races and lost both. Barry followed him around chanting, 'Loser, Loser.' Finally, Mark bloodied his nose. It ruined the day. After Phyllis passed away, I stopped trying to figure it out."

"There are a lot of ways you can go other than a simple outright equal division between them. You could put the money in trusts managed by a third party. You only have to decide, then we'll write it up for your signature."

⌘

T hat evening, Barry phoned. "Dad, I'd like to drop by for a few minutes if you're not busy."

"Fine. I've had dinner, and Mrs. Guerrero's gone. Give me an hour or so."

Exactly one hour later Barry appeared at the front door and let himself in. He went straight to the library where he knew his father was waiting. Dandridge was seated in a wingback chair in front of a stone fireplace with only a small flame. "This seems sufficient to take the chill off," he said.

"It feels good to me," said Barry, standing with his back to the fire. "I'll come straight to the point. We both know Mark can't handle money. His whole life he's never been able to hang onto a quarter. I don't think there's a cure for that, do you?"

"You're right. Mark doesn't handle money well, even in small amounts. You have a proposal?"

"This is just an idea, but what do you think about naming me Mark's trustee? You know I'm reliable when it comes to handling money. I'm not a spendthrift. I'll make sure Mark has at least as much income as you are giving us now, plus more if it seems appropriate."

"How do you think Mark would feel about having to look to you for his income?"

"You could stipulate a minimum amount to assure him an adequate income. That would leave it only partially in my control."

A loud banging sent both sets of eyes to the library's double doors. They flew open and in stalked Mark, eyes burning with anger. He sneered, "Just as I thought! When I saw your car in the driveway, I knew you were here, needling, getting your pitch in early, working your black magic. You never change!"

Barry said, "There's no question in the mind of anyone in this room who knows how to handle money! And it's not you, little brother."

Mark sprang towards Barry with his fist clenched. He drew back his arm as he grabbed Barry's collar.

"Stop it, Mark!"

Mark's bulging eyes and pursed lips said he had not heard his father's voice. Mark yelled, "I'll smash you to kingdom come! Get out of my life and stay out!"

"Mark! Stop! Sit down! Now!"

Mark shoved Barry into a chair. A lamp crashed to the floor and shattered. Barry sprang back and grabbed Mark's jacket. His face was red. He was nose to nose with Mark.

Dandridge jumped out of his chair and shouted, "Barry! Mark! Calm down. Just listen."

Berry let go, and Mark sat down, breathing heavily. His expression did not change. "Once a rat, always a rat!"

"Will you both listen? I have a few things to say to both of you."

Barry and Mark retreated to sofas, glaring at each other across a coffee table.

Dandridge returned to his chair and said, "I've been trying to think of a way, any way at all, to bring you two together. I don't know why you can't both act like adults. Why do you fight every time you're together?"

"Barry thinks he's God," Mark answered. He never does anything wrong. He turns off lights to save pennies. He lives with no style. He has to control everything, or he takes his marbles and goes home. He can't stand not being in charge."

"Right," countered Barry. "And you never do anything right. You don't take care of your money. You carouse your way around town, and your reputation isn't worth discussing."

"Maybe I'm not a number one citizen, but at least I have a life. I have fun. So what if I have a few fair-weather friends? Everybody does."

Dandridge spoke. "What I fear is that the day of my funeral will be the last day you set eyes on each other. Seeing you at odds when the family has always been important to your mother and me—I don't know if I can bear it."

"Dad, I apologize," Barry said. "We both love you. We want to do what mother would have wanted but face it. What separates us is money. We see possessions differently. We handle finances differently. In many ways," he said, "we're exact opposites."

"That's clearer to me now than it ever was," said Dandridge. "I'll have to sleep on it—if I can sleep at all," he said, raising his right hand to his temple. "I am tempted to say you two disgust me, but that's not the right word. I just feel sad. You run along now." His shoulders slumped. "Too much excitement has made me tired." His voice trailed off.

After Dandridge went upstairs, Barry and Mark sat silent. Mark's eyes lit up, and only the hint of a smile curved his lips. "You know, I played you like a violin when we were teenagers."

"How so?" asked Barry.

"When we left the campus to go to town and troll the girls, I always took you along. Do you know why?"

"Sure. Do you think I didn't know? You were more popular with the girls than I was, but you could only take one. That left all the others for me."

"Dog!"

"You used me. I used you," said Barry. "I guess we didn't fight about everything, did we?"

The following Sunday evening, Barry was waiting on the sidewalk when Dandridge arrived at the restaurant, remarking, "It's a bit chilly to be waiting out here."

"I didn't want to go in till you got here. If I did, Mark and I would be arguing by the time you came in. I thought the meal might be more peaceful with you present."

Mark was already looking over a menu when his father and Barry entered. He put the menu on the table and looked at them. His eyes squinted and his lips tightened. "Did you come together?"

Dandridge shook his head, "That question is uncalled for."

The meal was another five-star meal. The first topic, health, took up several minutes. They were all healthy. Dandridge checked his watch. Then came weather, including a possible trip to Aspen to get in some skiing. Another check of his watch told Dandridge they were more than halfway through their meal.

Food was their next item for discussion. They compared meals they had shared around the world to the meal they were now enjoying. This meal was right up there with the best. When dessert came, Dandridge was satisfied they would make it without any backbiting. Each had peach Melba, served at the moment of perfection.

"I must be dreaming," Dandridge said. "We've gone through an entire meal without a disagreement." He smiled. "There's hope yet." He rose to leave.

Mark said, "Dad, you always rush off. Stay for a while."

Dandridge hesitated. He looked at Mark, then at Barry. Barry nodded. A smile brought small dimples to Dandridge's cheeks. He slowly edged himself back into his chair to enjoy the rest of his coffee.

T uesday morning at 8:15, Barry's home phone rang and Grace answered. Her eyes widened, and she handed the phone to Barry. "It's your dad's housekeeper.

"Something's happened," Mrs. Guerrero said.

He listened a few seconds, then raced out of the house. His tires burned rubber as he sped away. Maneuvering traffic, he called Mark. Mark didn't answer.

"Mark, I hope you get this message soon. It's 8:20 and I'm on the way to Dad's. Mrs. Guerrero says something has happened to him. She's called 9-1-1."

Barry slammed on his brakes behind the emergency vehicle and dashed up the walk and through the open door. He took the stairs two at a time and rushed into his father's bedroom. Mrs. Guerrero stood at the side of the room holding her hands, tears in her eyes. Medics were working on Dandridge.

One of them said, "Sir, your father is non-responsive. We've done all we can for him." His father's hand felt cold to Barry.

"Do you want us to transport him to the hospital? Does he have a DNR?"

"I don't know. Take him to the hospital."

As Barry started toward the door, Mrs. Guerrero stopped him. "Mr. Dandridge gave me these papers and said I should give them to whoever comes—in case something happened to him."

She handed papers to Barry. The top paper was labeled DNR: Do Not Resuscitate. "Thank you, Mrs. Guerrero," Barry said and ran down the stairs to his car. He took off following the ambulance and again tried Mark's number. Mark picked up.

"Where's the fire?" he shouted into his phone. "Do you know what the hell time it is?"

"It's Dad. I'm following the ambulance to the hospital."

When Barry reached the hospital, Mark was already there, watching the EMTs transport Dandridge on a gurney to the emergency room.

"He looks bad," Mark said. "What happened?"

"I have no idea. I think he's gone." Tears slipped from his eyes.

Ten days later, Mark and Barry were ushered into an inner office of Gregg & Dennison Law Firm and offered leather upholstered chairs.

"Before we open the will, I'd like to say what a beautiful service your father had. I was not surprised the church was packed. Your dad has been an outstanding citizen, a generous benefactor to many charities and causes, and a kind and beloved individual. You have so much to be proud of."

"Thank you, Mr. Gregg. We're still feeling the loss. Dad had been ailing, but this was a surprise. I think we're still in a bit of a shock," said Barry.

"No one else is mentioned in the will besides you two, no siblings since your father was an only child, no nieces, or nephews. Your dad labored over his will. I think you'll find it's not ordinary in any sense of the word."

Barry and Mark looked at each other, puzzled. "Knowing our history, I can't imagine what he finally decided," Barry said. "He never shared it with us."

"The first stipulation is the simplest. Your present income will not change except for inflation. What you have been accustomed to receiving monthly you will continue to receive."

"That says nothing about the bulk of the estate. What will happen to it?" asked Mark.

"Your father has chosen a peculiar path. He and I had discussions about your strained relationship."

"An understatement," said Barry, "but I think we have found a little bit of common ground, so we won't be at each other's throats like we have been in the past. We just try to stay off certain subjects."

"I'm glad to hear that, and I think you'll be glad, too, once you hear your father's will. He talked about the creation stories in the Bible, the tale of two brothers. One became jealous and killed the other. When confronted with his deed, he asked the question, 'Am I my brother's keeper?' The implication was, 'No, I'm not.' But your father thinks he got it wrong."

"You're not going to preach a sermon, are you?" Mark said.

Morton smiled, "Rest assured, I won't. With that in mind, however, what your dad has placed in his will is that, other than your base allowances, which remain in place, neither of you will be able to control his inheritance until you are age 50.

"During the interim, the estate will be divided equally and placed in a trust. The unique provision is each of you will be the sole trustee of the estate of the other. Barry will manage your inheritance, Mark. Mark will manage yours, Barry. You must consult on every financial transaction that's made.

"You are both your brother's keeper for years into the future. This was your father's wish."

"That's weird," said Mark. "But," he added, "we can handle it, can't we, bro? I'll see you Sunday night."

If I Return

NFL pennants encircle the upper walls of the barbershop I patronize. Mirrors behind the barbers' chairs double the effect. The banter is almost always about sports. The barbers, and many of their customers as well, know who's on first, what's on second, and the genealogies and career histories of players and coaches, present and past.

I have few opinions about sports. So, imagine my surprise when I discovered my barber is a bird person. For some reason, I mentioned the bird feeders hanging in my backyard and it turned out, he has more feeders than I do, more kinds of feeders, and a birdbath. Plus, he feeds squirrels on his small patio, as I do. I told him the red-headed breed of hummingbirds is named Anna.

He said, "Yes, that's my mother's name and my girlfriend's name. It's the only kind of hummingbird we have here in the Valley." When I told him I had seen other species of hummingbirds, he was doubtful.

He'd seen songbirds attack hummingbirds feeding from the hummingbird feeders. My story about seeing an albino sparrow in my backyard impressed him.

He brushed the hair from my collar and removed the smock protecting my clothing. As I stood and reached for my hearing aids and glasses, a thought struck me. On my website, I have two poems about birds. He said he had no computer, so I offered him my phone and invited him to read, "If I Return."

The poem begins with *when*, not *if*. "When I die, *if* I return." I cling to the hope the reader doesn't reverse the order of the two words. Death has no *if*. The returning—that's the *if*. To some, returning might sound like reincarnation, when the soul or spirit returns after death in a new person or some other creature.

The second section of the poem focuses on how tough life is for a bird, facing dangers from weather and predators, and how they die unnoticed except perhaps by God.

The third section of the poem pictures the life of a bird as if the sky were an ocean where a bird can surf, sail, and ride the winds.

If I Return

After I die,
After my body is lowered into the grave,
Burnt into ashes,
Or fed to wild dogs,

If I return,
May it be as a bird.

Lifespan of months or years, no more,
Driven by season, snow, and storm,

Gleaning with never a Sabbath rest,
Falling to earth with none to mourn,

Banished from thought by all but God,
They sail on placid lakes of blue,

Fly with full-feathered wings,
Swim in heaven's crystal vault,

Split clear skies without a sound,
Surf invisible winds and clouds.

Bound by nature's laws alone,
They soar . . .
And soar . . .
And soar . . .

After I die, if I return,
May it be as a bird.

My barber read the poem while I prepared to leave.
When he turned to give me my phone, he had tears in
his eyes. "Man," he said, almost breathless. "Thanks."

Also by Wayland Bryant Jackson

When God Disappeared...and Where God Turned Up, 2022, a Memoir. Available now wherever books are sold.

Visit my website:

https://waylandjackson.com/

If you feel like responding
to any of my writings,
please email me:

jacksonwayland48@gmail.com

I will write back.

Coming Soon on Amazon!

A Book of Poetry: Do Not Marry for Love

INSIDE . . . *Do Not Marry for Love*

Do not marry for love.
Like the tide, love flows and ebbs.
Like a selfish toddler, it's never satisfied.
Like a fire, fuel spent, it dies out.

Do not marry for love.
Like a fever, love will overcome you.
Like the awe of Christmas time
When only the wrappings remain.

Do not marry for love.
You are not "prince and princess."
No one lives "happily ever after."
Love does not conquer all.

Marry her for the light in her eyes,
The reflection of the sun through her hair,
Her intoxicating smell, her beguiling smile.
Marry her for the shape of her hands.

Marry her for the tip of her nose,
Marry her for the warmth in her voice,
Marry her because you match,
Because she is strong.

Then comes love
That knows neither tide nor season,
That will not go away; that needs no stoking,
And blankets the soul like a snowy benediction.

About the Author

Wayland Bryant Jackson, born in 1931 in southern Oklahoma, migrated to California in 1952. Married 62 years to Betty Jane Hollandsworth Owens (1930 – 2016), they had five loving children, six grandchildren, and seven great-grands. A graduate of Oklahoma Baptist University and Golden Gate Baptist Theological Seminary, Wayland is a retired public school teacher living in Fresno, CA.

www.ingramcontent.com/pod-product-compliance
Lightning Source LLC
Chambersburg PA
CBHW031318170626
46807CB00002B/467